A Boss and His Rider:

A Chicago Love Affair

Domaneque Banks

Author's Note

This is a republication, previously titled A Chicago Hood Love.

Dedication

This novel is dedicated to anyone who has ever been told that they can't accomplish something, that they can't believe in themselves and that they are able unable to make their dreams possible. For years, I struggled with not having enough faith in myself to make my dreams a reality. This book is the proof that dreams do come true and that no matter how many people don't believe in you there is always that one person who truly does! Thank You!

Prologue

"Please don't kill me!!!" Louie screamed frantically. Adonis stared at him with no pity in his eyes, "Shut the fuck up!!", He roared back.

If it was anything that Adonis hated the most it was a fucking thief. Adonis King was the head of the of The Dynasty, the biggest drug empire in Chicago. For 10 years, he ran the business for his father Derrick King who was now unable to walk due to being shot more than 7 years ago in a drug bust gone wrong. Being one of the biggest drug pins in Chicago led Adonis to make some drastic choices. He didn't wanna have to kill Louie, but somebody had been stealing product and money from them. Thanks to his long-time partner Truth, they finally knew it was Louie. Adonis had to admit, he tried to cover his tracks well, but he just wasn't good enough. When every crook thinks they're getting away with something, they always leave behind a messy trail. Pressing the gun to his skull, Adonis was in rage. He knew Louie since he was a child, and never for once would he have thought he would betray him or his father like this.

"I knew you was a snake ass nigga." Truth said looking at Louie dead in his eyes. "

"Bitch I told you I ain't steal from ya'll! The fuck I look like? I can get own bread!" Louie said trying to sound like he wasn't scared the nigga was terrified. He knew that Derrick didn't play about his money which is why he would never take from him.

Punching him in the mouth with the butt of the gun, blood poured from Louie's mouth like a faucet. "We don't trust your ass!" Adonis said sitting across from Louie. "You the only one who was responsible for taking all the profit to the bank. Nigga I run Chicago did you not think me or my father would notice all the missing money? As much product as we been shipping out of this motherfucker? You really thought you would get off with more than 60'gs and nobody would miss that shit? I should cut your fuckin' tongue out your mouth for all the lies you spewing!" Adonis said! He was past done with hearing Louie's lies and excuses. He wanted to take this nigga out so bad it made his dick hard. "Any final words?" Adonis said putting the trigger inside Louie's bloody mouth.

Louie looked Adonis in the eyes and shot him a bird. The tears rolled down his cheeks as he knew he would never see the faces of his wife and kids ever again. Adonis felt just as bad as Louie. He didn't wanna end his life, but he had broken the code. He knew Louie ever since he was two years old. Now the nigga who he had admired ever since he was a child was about to pay for the consequences of his shitty choices with his life. BAM! BAM! Shooting twice inside Louie's mouth, his skull shattered into a thousand pieces, and blood was splattered everywhere. Louie's body fell back.

"Call my pops and tell him the shit is done with!" Adonis snapped. "You and you," he said pointing at the workers, "Ya'll clean this shit up. Truth, I want this body gone. Take one of the cars out back and go out of Chicago tonight", He said handing Truth 5g's. This should be enough to take care of everything. hit my line sometime tomorrow and let me know everything went smooth." Adonis said about to jump inside the warehouse shower. Even though Louie was dead, it still didn't sit well with him. The way he pleaded and begged for him to spare his life. Trying to shrug it, off he instantly thought of his old lady Imani. After a crazy ass day, she was the only medicine he needed to cure all of the sick thoughts in his head.

Chapter 1

Imani tossed and turned in her satin white sheets. Looking over at the clock, she noticed it was going on 3 am, and Adonis still hadn't returned home. Not wanting to seem overly anxious, she immediately decided to calm her thoughts by taking a hot shower. Taking off her Chanel black lace robe, she stood in front of the mirror and removing her matching bra and panty set. Instantly, Imani wished that Adonis was there to hold her in his strong arms.

As Imani stood in the mirror, she couldn't help but to admire herself. She was no doubt a beautiful woman. She had jet black hair so long it flowed down past her waist. Her honey brown skin complexion went well with her brown eyes. Adonis always told her they reminded him of the finest chocolate diamonds he had ever seen, especially when she looked into the sun. As she stepped into the water, she let it run all over her body. She rubbed her chocolate nipples and moaned aloud from the delight. Closing her eyes, she rubbed her clit and began imagining that Adonis was eating her pussy with his full lips. He would devour her pussy, and she would melt into his mouth with each tongue stroke. Lost in a trance, she didn't even notice that Adonis had stepped into the shower behind her. He quickly removed her hands and replaced them with his along her ample breast and wet pussy.

Caught off guard but pleasantly surprised, Imani was lost in the moment. As he rubbed his curved dick against her fat ass, her juices immediately began to pour. The wetness that escaped her lips couldn't be denied. Craving to taste her, Adonis got on his knees and threw her right leg over his broad shoulders. He had been waiting all night to taste her honey pot. Her sweet pussy was just right. The more he stroked her with his tongue, the fatter and wetter her pussy became.

Imani couldn't take it anymore. The pleasure was enough for her to scream. She had to have him inside of her. Turning off the shower, he picked her up by her waist and pinned her against the shower wall as he entered her slowly. His eyes rolled to the back of his head everytime he entered her warm insides. It felt like the first time he made love to her. Holding her tightly in his arms, he moaned deeply in her ear, "Baby shit you feel so good."

"Ooh daddy... God this dick feels so good," Imani moaned while scratching his back. The strokes were becoming so intense she started to black out from the pleasure. No one could fuck her like Adonis. He knew her body, like he was created just to please her. Adonis couldn't even front, he was so far gone over Imani.

Images from the nights' previous events were starting to take over his mind. As he thought of Louie lying in a pool of blood, he started to stroke Imani even harder. Her pussy couldn't take anymore. Imani could feel his dick all the way in her stomach. It throbbed each time he thrusted into her warm insides.

"Baby I'm about to cum all over your dick ugh I love you!" Imani screamed aloud from the pleasure she was feeling with each stroke.

Adonis wanted to tell her he loved her back, but he kept seeing the face of the man that he killed tonight. His eyes, the way his body layed lifelessly, and the way he pleaded for his life before he pulled the trigger kept replaying over and over in his head. Pounding harder and harder, Imani was screaming really loud from the mixture of pain and pleasure the dick was giving to her.

"Baby OMG YES Fuck me!", She grunting loudly. Adonis let his love escape into her warmth.

"Damn!", She sighed breathing heavily. "You haven't done that in a while. I love you. You know that right?" Imani said kissing her man deeply.

Stepping out the shower and into the bedroom, she noticed Adonis was in a trance sitting on the edge of the bed. "Babe you good?" She questioned.

"Yeah I'm okay baby come lay down." Adonis said.

Lying next to her, he held her from behind. He tried to erase the images from tonight out of his head. "Baby can you promise me something?" Adonis said. Turning around to face him, she said "Anything."

"Promise that no matter what that you gonna always rock with a nigga. I know I ain't perfect, but I do love you. You got my heart. I just need to know that you gonna always be here." Adonis said staring deeply into Imani's eyes.

Seeing the anguish in his eyes, she stroked his face. "Baby where am I going? You are me and I am you. Ain't nobody going nowhere." She said kissing his sweet lips. He held her in his arms and they both fell into a deep sleep.

Adonis King was up before the sun came up reflecting on his life. For the past couple of days and weeks, he kept trying to come up with the words to say to his father. He had finally made the decision that he was ready to leave the game. It had been a long 10 year run, but now he felt like it was coming to an end. He didn't wanna let his pops down, but he didn't want to become him either. Derrick King was 52 years old, chocolate, and just as sexy as Adonis without dreads. They both shared the same dark eyes, but inside Derrick was a cold, ruthless, and bitter man. The fact that Adonis' momma had run out on them shortly after he was born had damaged his heart. The only things he loved were his business, his money and his son. As far as he was concerned, these bitches were only good for busting nuts on their fat asses, and he would never trust another one with his heart. After becoming handicapped from a drug bust gone wrong, he still tried to help Adonis with what he could. He left his son to be the head person in charge of his empire. He had no choice but to depend on him. The Chicago streets had been Derricks home since he was 5 years old. He knew the territories like the back of his hand.

He started selling dope on street corners and alleys when he was a little boy. By the time he was 16, he was claiming his respect in the streets and eventually became one of the biggest drug pins in the city. The fact that he couldn't walk really fucked with Derricks head. He knew that he held no true power without the ability to walk his own streets, so rightfully he handed down everything that his blood, sweat, and tears built to his only son.

Since Adonis was young, he never had to want for anything. His father had always looked out for him. He had taught him how to be a man without knowing a mother's love or touch. He struggled emotionally growing up as he tried to express the feelings he harbored inside with his pops. He wouldn't allow it. Derrick saw weakness in showing emotion, especially over shit that didn't matter. If it wasn't affecting his pockets, then why cry over it. Any love that he felt for his estranged wife left and ran out on him and his son. As far he was concerned, she was a useless bitch who abandoned her family. Derrick couldn't understand why Adonis still longed for her. He made sure to let his son know that he didn't wanna hear shit about his mom's period.

Just as he became lost in thought, Adonis' cellphone started to ring. It was his partner Truth.

"What up?" Adonis answered.

"Aye bruh, we need to get up. I think I fucked up on

something can you meet Asap?"

"Let me get myself together. A nigga just really waking up give me about an hour."

"Ok cool 1." Truth replied hanging up.

Adonis wondered what had Truth so hyped up. As long as he known him, he barely ever lost his way or fucked up anything when it came to The Dynasty. Truth was always on point with his shit, and that's why his pops fucked with him hard also.

Truth was Adonis' right hand man. From selling their first pound of cocaine, to getting their first piece of pussy together, they had known each other forever. Besides Imani, Truth was the only other person to know all of Adonis's hidden secrets. Along with the fact that he had no other living siblings, to Adonis Truth was like his brother in every sense of the word. The bond they shared ran deep.

Making his way back into the living room from the balcony, he saw Imani near the kitchen bar preparing breakfast. She looked beautiful as hell in a white tank top and her boy shorts. Her ass sat perfectly in the crevices. Her jet black hair was in a simple ponytail. No makeup adorned her baby doll face; she was perfection without it. Adonis couldn't help but to admire her.

"What you cheesing so hard for?" She asked.

"You just look gorgeous this morning." Adonis complimented.

"Well after the way you put it on me last night, I can't help but to glow. So bae I was thinking, we have breakfast and spend the whole day together. Just us. We can have lunch and do some shopping and go check a movie out."

"Damn ma, I can't today. I gotta meet up with Truth in an hour."

"Really Adonis!?" Imani sucked her teeth, throwing

the pan back into the cabinet. "You was just out last night. Does it always have to be about business? We never just chill anymore. You honestly pay the streets more attention than do your own woman. Like wtf? If you really my man you need to act like it because all this missing in action shit is for the birds!" Imani yelled.

"What the fuck is that supposed to mean?!" Adonis spewed becoming irritated. "I'm working. You know I hate doing this shit, but you don't complain when the fucking money comes in. Fancy cars, shopping sprees, your wardrobe and our lifestyle ... that shit ain't gonna pay for itself Imani. You need to chill with all that shit you talking!"

"No you need to chill. You call this working? The fuck Adonis! You are a fucking drug dealer. That's not a legit job. You think money and shopping sprees can make up for all the missed time we haven't spent together but I'm tired! Tired of loving a man who is in love with the game more than his rider. I had my own before I met you Adonis. I don't need all this lavish shit to make me happy. I want you!!" Imani shot back hurting Adonis' feelings.

"I'm tired of lying awake at night worried if you gonna come back home or be dead in these cold streets. All I want is for you and me to live a normal life. Why can't that be enough for you man?" She finished.

Not knowing what to say, all Adonis did was stare at her. He knew she was only telling the truth. Continuing to pour her heart out to him, she started to cry. Imani was so upset.

"I never wanted you to put yourself at risk, especially not for your father. Adonis he doesn't give a fuck about you. He got you in the middle of his bullshit, risking your life over and over again for his choices!" Imani ranted.

She had given all of herself to Adonis, she hated to see him be used, especially by someone who claimed to love him. The thought of losing him was enough for her to lose her mind.

Adonis was all that she truly knew. No man had ever looked out for her or loved her the way that he did. Growing up without a father or mother, Adonis was her only family. Since she was 5, she had been in out of foster homes and grew with no true support system. When she was 19, she finally decided to leave Oklahoma and start her whole life over in Chicago. All the guys she had met before Adonis only used her, beat her and took her for granted. With Adonis, it was completely different. He valued her mind before her body, and he truly cared for her best interest at heart. In him, she had found her best friend and her lover all rolled into one.

"Baby I'm sorry." Adonis started.

"Naw, you not sorry," Imani said still angry. "If you were truly sorry, you would call Truth and tell him that you can't come thru. We really need to talk. To be real, I'm not feeling this anymore. I'm tired of this shit. You say you wanna change and be legit then prove it. I'm fed up with the broken promises and excuses!"

"Imani do you think I honestly wanna do this shit forever? I'm trying to provide for us! A nigga wanna do right by you, but I can't just up and leave. I can't just abandon my pops like that. He needs somebody that he can trust to run The Dynasty, someone that can keep the streets on lock. He already can't walk and if I'm not there, then who else gonna be able to hold him down?!"

Becoming more pissed Imani cut him off all she could was shake her head, "That's not your problem or your damn job. "You always trying to look out for your damn daddy, but when you were doing charges for his ass did he look out for you?! He damn sure didn't value your life when you took that sentence for him or when you took them three bullets for him. Your ass is lucky to still even be alive!!" Imani screamed.

"Yo, that's enough Imani. Now my father may be a lot of things, but he still raised me alone with no help. All we had was one another. He may not show it, but I know that nigga loves me." Adonis explained.

"Please! I'm the one who loves you Adonis! I'm the one who looks out for you. When you did a two year bid, who held you down? I did! Your father only came to visit you twice so how the hell is that love?!" Imani kept tearing in Adonis about his shady ass father.

Adonis couldn't handle Imani when she was snapping. It was like talking to a brick wall. Once she was mad, it was no calming her down. The more shit she talked, the more aggravated he had become. Not wanting to blow up on her, he stood up to leave.

"Look we can talk about this later. I'm out." Adonis said getting up to leave.

"You always gone or out so fuck it leave. Every time I try to get through to you, it falls on deaf ears anyway!" She screamed as she slammed the door in his face.

All Imani could do was burst into tears. Slumping onto the floor, she felt defeated. She hated fighting with him. All she wanted to do was save him, hell, save their relationship. She hated the fact that every time they talked about his business, he would just become fed up and walk out. Nothing would ever get solved that way. How could they ever change their situation if he couldn't communicate his feelings? All she knew was that she tired of hearing the same lies, and she was tired of wishing for a new life that would never happen. For the past five years that Imani knew Adonis, it was mostly because of the disagreements of what he did for a living that caused a rift between them. Sure the lavish trips and shopping sprees were nice, but the risk of having it all because of the dangerous life that Adonis led wasn't worth the risk.

If giving up the glitz and glam was what she had to

do in order to keep her man alive and safe with her then so be it. She could sacrifice all the material shit.

"Okay get it together girl", Imani said to herself as she stood up and wiped her tears. She decided right then and there she was gonna boss up and stop crying over spilt milk. Stressing her herself to death wasn't gonna fix shit either. Plus, she was too beautiful to be looking haggard and old when she was so young. Looking over at the kitchen table, she realized they hadn't even touched the breakfast that she had prepared. She had thrown down with the cheese eggs, French toast, waffles, turkey bacon, and her famous fruit smoothies.

"I'll be damned if all this food goes to waste," Imani whispered under her breath. Deciding she really needed to vent, she called her one and only girlfriend in Chicago; Nyla.

Now one thing Imani didn't do was fuck with a lot of bitches. Females were shiesty. She saw that a lot growing up. She knew it couldn't be all of them, but most females had shady or grimy ass ways. She knew all too well just how bitches could smile in your face, but try to replace you in a minute; especially now that she was with a good man like Adonis.

With Nyla shit was different. She had met her when she first came to Chicago and didn't have a job or have a place to stay. Nyla was the one to help her get on her feet. Imani knew without a doubt she could trust her, especially since she had a steady relationship with a nigga she knew forever named Troy. Imani knew for a fact that she would never try to betray her or fuck her over. She was the truth. Despite her relationship with Adonis, she needed that one female that she could party and kick it with. Every chick needed a fun girl to turn up with, and in Nyla Imani had just that

"Heyyy boo! What you doing?" Nyla answered on

the fifth ring. It always took her forever to pick up her phone.

"Hey Ny. What you doing? Come fuck with me. I just made breakfast, come eat with me," Imani stated while biting a piece of bacon.

"Chile I was just about to head to I-hop with Troy for breakfast. Where is Adonis? Is everything cool?" Nyla asked. "Dang my fault I figured you would already be booked." she chuckled lightly,"

"It's straight. I'll just get up with you another time."

"You better wake that nigga up of yours to eat with you. I know he busy being Mr. Big Executive but long nights come with early mornings." Ny said.

"Yeah I guess." Imani's voice drifted off into the distance.

She wished she could just open up to Nyla and tell her what Adonis really did for a living, and what his long nights truly consisted of. Shit, a bitch was tired of keeping all this shit in. The problem was she didn't know just how much information she could trust Nyla with. That type of information, she had to be careful who she shared it with. She couldn't let her know all the tea. If they ever fell out she might rat her man out and then Adonis could go right back to prison.

"Imani aye you sure you good?" Nyla asked again.

"Yeah I'll be okay. Go ahead and have fun with your baby daddy."

"Girl I am over here laughing so damn hard." Ny said while dying laughing. "Bitch ain't no kids in this belly. But for real, if you need me I'll come over and cancel with Troy." Nyla could tell that her home-girl was off.

"Well yeah if you can come thru I need to vent." Imani finally admitted.

"Okay boo here I come. See you in 20." Ny said

hanging up and preparing to head to Imani.

Placing her cell phone back on the kitchen counter, Imani started to relax, she hoped that when Adonis returned that he would at least start to come to his senses, and have a clear head. Maybe he would even reconsider leaving The Dynasty. Truth be told, she didn't know how much more she could take. She didn't know how long they would last if he didn't change his mind. Only time would tell.

Chapter 2

Pulling into the warehouse parking lot, Adonis was still pissed. He was tired of killing, selling drugs, and working for his father Derrick. Did Imani have to constantly put pressure on him? He knew he had to figure out a way to get out, but how? The last thing he wanted to do was let his pops down. Stepping out of his all red 2016 Ferrari, Adonis was stressing but damn sure didn't look like how he felt. He donned an all-white Tee with his true religion jeans and his all white forces. His long dreads were pulled back into a ponytail. The white blazer he rocked set his outfit all the way off.

Noticing him pulling up, Truth walked outside to greet him, "Wat up bruh?"

"I'm good what was so urgent that you needed to see me so soon? You know I was chilling with my ole lady." Adonis said irritated.

"I know my fault but I just wanted to settle some business from last night. Thought that was taken care of?" Truth said as Adonis looked confused.

The whole point of taking out Louie was because he had been stealing most of the profit for the last 6 months. They had been trying to pinpoint who it could be, and all evidence led to Louie. The blow had hurt Derrick the most. He was one of the first niggas to start The Dynasty up with him, and he had been his right hand man. Not to mention he had known Adonis since he was kid.

"I think we took out the wrong dude fam." Truth suddenly spit it out.

"What you mean Truth? Who the fuck else would have stolen from us if it wasn't Louie?" Adonis said through clenched teeth. He was hot!

"I don't know man I'm just as confused as you! I realized after I counted up the last shipment from last night that money is still coming up short. Money that couldn't have been in Louie's possession." Truth explained.

Adonis was in rage. Not only had they killed the wrong man, but someone that was around them was a fucking thief. He hated thieves with a passion. Even more, he hated a nigga that was greedy.

"Fuck! Nigga you said you was fucking sure. You told me and pops you was sure it was Louie. If you knew you wasn't sure I would have never knocked his ass off." Adonis said starting to feel guilty. "He pleaded and begged me to believe that he wouldn't steal from us, but listening to you and pops, a nigga who helped raised me is dead!! Yo, I'm telling you now Truth if what you telling me is true, his blood is on your hands not mine!"

Adonis was so mad he couldn't even think straight. He had felt guilty as hell for killing Louie. All night he had tossed and turned because it didn't sit right with him. To find this out only made him feel worse. Feeling the rage that was building up within him, he threw Truth up against the cold, gray warehouse wall, "The fuck is your problem bruh? Nigga you had me take out the wrong mothafucka'. I've known Louie my whole damn life since I was a child. He had a wife and kids. Trying to be fucking loyal to ya'll, I took away an innocent man's life. Fuck, Fuck, Fuck!" he roared.

Seeing Adonis this angry hurt Truth to his core. He had never meant for this to happen. He thought for sure it was Louie who was stealing from them all this time. He had never seen Adonis so destroyed over taking somebody out. He hated to see him beat himself up about it. The anguish was written all over his face. He knew that he was furious at him right now, but all Truth wanted to do was what he always wanted to do for the past 8 years, and that was to have Adonis for himself.

He knew that Adonis saw him as a brother and a friend, but somehow over the years he had fallen deeply in love with him. He was so sick of denying his feelings. Watching him be with someone else, let alone a stuck up bitch like Imani, it was sickening to him to have to see the two of them together. Imani could never love him the way he could. Truth knew about the secrets that Adonis carried with him from The Dynasty. They stood side by side watching each-others backs, taking out enemies, making major moves and running Chicago together. Truth tried to hide his affections by messing with multiple women. Trying to fuck away the desires of a man that he knew he could probably never have.

"Adonis look, I'm sorry I fucked up. Imma fix this shit." Truth explained.

Letting him go, Adonis looked around the warehouse disgusted. Not only with himself, but with everything surrounding him. Imani had been right the whole time. This shit his father created was causing him nothing but pain and worry. Because of him, he held the blood of so many lives on his hands. He was tired of pretending that he was built for this shit.

"I'm getting out. I can't take this shit anymore," Adonis declared.

"Now you talking crazy." Truth replied. "Ain't no way you giving all this up Adonis. This is the dream bruh. You own these streets. Niggas fear you..." Truth continued before Adonis cut him off.

"Man fuck all of that. This is what my father built. This his dream. His whole life had been about The Dynasty. It left him crippled and he still won't let it go. I even did a two year bid for him." Adonis said tired.

Truth couldn't believe his ears. The man that he loved was really talking about leaving the business. Never in a million years he would think that that he would give it all up. In a way Truth felt betrayed. Not only had he put his life on the line for The Kings, but he had put his all into the Dynasty. Truth had invested and protected Derrick and Adonis since Adonis took over for his pops, so to hear this was so unlike him. Putting two and two together, he knew the one and only person that could make Adonis want to do something so stupid was Imani.

"That bitch got you all twisted." Truth stated not realizing his thoughts flowed from out of his mouth.

"Yo what you say?" Adonis stated walking towards Truth.

"I said the only reason you wanna fuck up everything now is for that bitch Imani. She gonna be your downfall bruh." Truth's face was all twisted up and the anger was written all over his face.

"Who the fuck you calling a bitch? Imani gotta be all that just because she wants better for me? Or is it because she not thirsty like the bitches you mess with?" Adonis said laughing.

"Adonis the bitch is stuck up. Ever since you met her, she been a big ass distraction. You wasn't thinking about leaving till she got all in yo head. You know good and damn well your pops ain't gonna trust no one else to run this shit but you, so you might as well dead all that G." Truth shot back.

"Real talk this shit is for the birds. You brought me down here thinking you had to tell me some minor shit when only you just wanted to tell me that you fucked up on your end!" Adonis snarled.

"Who fucked up!?" Both turning their heads towards the voice that distracted them, in rolled Derrick King with his assistant and personal mistress, Mya. "What ya'll in here bitching about? I know two grown ass men not in their feelings." Derrick stated.

"We need to talk alone. Truth, Mya can ya'll give us a minute." Adonis demanded.

Not wanting to leave his side, Truth followed Mya unwillingly to the other side of the warehouse.

Speak ya mind son. Just as he thought the words would fly out, Adonis found himself fumbling. It was now or never. If anything, he wasn't no punk and he wasn't scared to tell his father shit.

"I don't think running The Dynasty is for me anymore." Adonis blurted out.

Derrick was looking at his son with astonishment. "What do you mean? How the fuck you going to betray me like this?" Derrick stated hurt.

"For 10 years, I have done all you have asked of me. I mean shit, I even did a two year bid for you!" Adonis shot back to his father.

"You knew the risk when I got gunned down. You told me you had my back. I trusted you to run my business and only you because I thought you were different then these other punk ass niggas on the streets! Instead you letting the pussy control you. Ever since you met Imani she been getting inside your head. You have let that bitch manipulate your life. She even got you to betray your own flesh and blood. I told you never let pussy control your emotions. You fucking up Adonis!" Derrick scolded him.

First let me check you real quick, Imani ain't no bitch. The same bitch you talking about held me down more than your ass did when I got sent to the pen." Adonis said defending Imani and calling Derrick out on his shit at the same time.

"I had business to handle." Derrick replied.

"And what is it that's more important to you than your son, your child!" Adonis shouted.

"Nigga you ain't a baby. You're a grown ass man. You should've just charged it to the game!!" Derrick said in a tone filled with no emotion at all.

Adonis stood in shock. He knew his father was cold hearted, but the least he could do was show sympathy towards his son.

"That's always been the difference between me and you Adonis. You're so weak hearted, a punk. If you weren't such a bitch you would have the mindset to take the legacy further than what you have. I have always tried to tell you these bitches ain't shit. All they do is suck you dry. They destroy you! Fuck them and move on, but never let them get your heart. You failed and now you gonna let this bitch destroy what we built!" Derrick shouted.

"You built this shit!" Adonis roared. "I looked out for you because you became handicapped, useless. You became weak in your own line of business, or whatever the fuck you think this is." Adonis said hitting below the belt.

Derrick was heated at this point. He knew that if nothing else would set him off, it would be the fact that he couldn't walk or take charge. Just the thought of him having to depend on everyone else destroyed his ego in every sense of the word. Rolling up to Adonis in his wheelchair, he looked at him square in the eyes.

"Now nigga I suggest you watch what the fuck you say. Don't forget I made you the man that you are today. Don't let this chair fool you, I still call the shots and don't you ever forget that shit. I'll die before I let you disrespect me." Derrick threatened.

"You disrespected me and my woman, so tell me why the hell should I respect you? Like I said I'm done with this shit. I'm a grown ass man and just like I chose to help you, I'm choosing now to leave. 10 years ago I didn't have Imani. I love her and she worth more to me than all this bullshit. So you can have it fuck it all." Adonis screamed.

For a moment it was complete silence. All you could hear was the trucks that rode by on the interstate. The tension was so thick in the air that a knife couldn't even cut through it.

A father and son who once only had each other were suddenly at odds. Adonis finally spoke, breaking the silence.

"We can square away the last of my affairs by the end of the week. I'm about to be out.

Shaking his head, all Derrick could do was laugh. "You really think it's gonna be that simple? Did you think that the Almighty Derrick King would just let you off the hook just like that? You think just because you're my son that you gonna get some special privileges mothafucka? You crazy if you think you gonna walk out on me like your punk ass mother." Derrick stated become delusional.

In a rage, Adonis charged at his father knocking him backwards out of his wheelchair.

"Don't ever speak about my mother like she's one of your fucking whores!" Adonis screamed.

Hearing the commotion, Truth and Mya ran to see what was going on. "Yo chill! What the fuck is wrong with you?" Truth said trying to hold Adonis back. He looked sexy as fuck to him when got mad, and Truth loved it but he didn't show it on the outside.

"Baby are okay?" Mya asked trying to help Derrick up.

"Bitch I'm fine get off of me!" Derrick yelled taking his anger out on Mya. In shock, Mya just stared back at him. She was only trying to help. "Truth come help me up." Derrick ordered.

Truth helped him up in his wheelchair. Pissed and fed u,p he looked at Adonis with nothing but rage in his eyes. "Get out of my warehouse! Just know this shit isn't over by a long shot." Derrick promised. Rolling into his office he slammed the door shut behind him.

"I'm up." Adonis told Truth,

"Man can we just talk this out." Truth pleaded.

"Bruh ain't nothing else to say I'm done with it. I ain't got shit else to say to that man." Grabbing his car keys, Adonis left Truth and Mya standing alone.

Truth knew he had to figure out a way to fix this shit. It was no way he was losing his friend and the man that he loved to that bitch Imani. If Adonis was truly done with The Dynasty, he would cut anything and everyone associated with it including him. It was no way that he was gonna lose Adonis that easily. Not over his dead body.

Chapter 3

Imani was standing in her closet trying to decide what outfit she was gonna rock tonight for the club. She was overjoyed and ecstatic to finally be getting out of the house. After 2 and a half hours, she found the perfect outfit to compliment her long jet black curls. She opted for a white Versace mini dress with matching 6-inch heels and her diamond earrings. Hoping Adonis would make it home in time to go out with her, Lyla, and Troy, she eagerly anticipated his surprise. For the past couple of days, he kept saying he had something big to tell her. Imani had been so anxious and nervous to find out what it could be. She had no idea what Adonis could have up his sleeve.

"Aye bae I'm back." Adonis stated.

"I'm upstairs getting dressed boo." Imani replied.

Upon him entering the doorway, Imani bit her bottom lip. Damn her man was so fucking fine.

"Imma change my clothes too." Adonis stated.

"Why baby? You look good in what you got on." Imani complimented. It was true Adonis looked handsome in an all-black Tee with black jeans and his gold and black forces and shades. His long dreads framed his face and hung long and crinkly all over his head. Imani was in awe. He looked like a chocolate god.

"Bae you fine just the way you are." She said kissing him. Making the kiss deeper, his dick started to get rock hard.

"Hold up you keep fucking with a nigga like that we ain't gonna make it to the club. Shit we can set our own party off right here in the bedroom." Adonis said joking.

"Ha-Ha, very funny. We going out." Imani replied.

"This was your idea in the first place and we haven't been out in weeks." Imani complained.

"Calm down Ma. We going out but damn you making it hard for a nigga to keep calm in that outfit." Imani looked gorgeous. He knew that one day he had to make her his wife. He couldn't wait to see her face glow when he would finally tell her that he dropped The Dynasty. Even though his father was still threatening him, he didn't give a damn. In his eyes, he was done with it for good this time.

Truth had been blowing up his phone ever since that night, but Adonis didn't feel like talking. Once he stated how he felt, he wasn't gonna go back and explain himself to nobody.

"You ready bae?"

"Yes." Imani replied putting the finishing touches on her makeup.

They chose to ride out in Adonis's all black 2016 charger. If they were gonna pull up to Studio Paris Nightclub, they had to come thru in style. It was one of the hottest nightclubs in Chicago. All of the relevant music artist and stars were there frequently when they came to town, and tonight would be no different. It was Saturday night and the place was gonna be packed. Adonis knew just the perfect spot inside the club to make his announcement to Imani. Riding through the Chicago streets blasting Panda by Desiigner, Imani couldn't help but to admire the club as they pulled up. The club was beautiful with bright lights. Two lines were wrapped around the building, one for VIP, and one for regular guest. You could hear the music blasting from the inside. Rolling into the valet, Imani couldn't help but to notice that Adonis' phone had been ringing and going off since they left the house. He didn't bother to answer it like he normally would when they were driving. She immediately suspected some shit was up. Not wanting to ruin the night, she decided not to trip about it for now. Her and her man hadn't been out in a good minute since he had been so busy. She just wanted them to have a good time tonight with her friends.

"Welcome to Club Paris Mr. King." The valet attendant greeted them with a smile. "I'll take your keys for you." Handing him the keys Imani waited to be escorted out of the car.

Grabbing her man's hand, she and Adonis made their way inside the club. All the bitches were staring Adonis down and Imani was unbothered. She didn't pay them hoes any mind, she knew her man was fine, and that none of them females could equal up to the solid woman that she was. Hell Adonis wasn't worried about them anyway. He was mad aggravated. Truth kept texting and calling his phone every 15 mins. He was trying to figure out what the hell could be so urgent that he had to blow up his phone so heavy. If anything, niggas knew Adonis hated talking on the phone anyway, he was more of a face to face type of man.

The VIP section of the club was lit. Strippers were dancing on the poles, the bar was full, and Adonis loved it. He was out with his woman enjoying life like he should be. All the wealthiest niggas in the city were waiting to spend their hard earned money on drinks and the bitches. Sitting in VIP smoking a fat ass blunt was Troy sitting next to Nyla. Troy was sexy as hell. He had a low cut with waves, a full beard, and milk chocolate skin. He had the most seductive smile, and when he cheesed his pearly white teeth would show. Him and Nyla made the perfect match. She was 5'3 with short black hair, flawless caramel skin, and her cat like eyes made everyone say she resembled the actress Nia Long. Tonight she was rocking a black mini dress, and red heels, she looked gorgeous!

"Yasssss bitch! You are rocking that dress." Imani

complimented her friend.

"You look good too bihhh. Between me you, we the only two baddies in here tonight." Ny stated confidently.

As they ladies were chatting it up, Adonis dapped up Troy.

"Wat up fam. What's good?" Adonis said greeting Troy. They weren't the best of friends. They didn't run in the same circles, but they did get along since they double dated with the ladies a lot. Adonis admired Troy. The nigga had a legit business, never was in any trouble from what he could see, and he loved and respected his woman. Adonis wanted to fuck with him more now that he was trying to become clean from his dirty dealings in the streets. Knowing that he was gonna have to take Imani in private soon, to make his announcement. Adonis was nervous as fuck. What better way to calm his nerves and turn shit up than by getting some drink's?

"Aye ya'll drinks on me tonight." Adonis announced. The beautiful waitress with the fat ass brought over a bottle of Hennessey and Tequila Shots with a bunch of the finest liquor from the bar. Believe it or not, Imani was nervous too.

"Girl you straight?" Nyla asked.

"Adonis said he needs to tell me something tonight. I don't know what it could be?" Imani said lost.

"OMG Imani duh!" Nya exclaimed.

Looking at Nyla confused, Imani replied, "Girl What?"

"He gonna ask you to marry him. Hell ya'll been together long enough." Ny rationalized.

"You really think so!?" Imani had been on go all night about Adonis' phone ringing off the hook, and just about what he had to tell her. She never even considered the fact that Adonis may just pop the question. Chugging down a shot of tequila she became antsy. "What if he really asks me? Omg I'm not even dressed right and we at the club of all places." She said shaking her head. Imani shut up you look beautiful ain't this what you been what you been wanting? Hell yeah! Nothing would make me happier than to become Mrs. Imani King. Deep down she knew she wanted to be married, but she also knew what being married to a drug dealer would mean. She knew she would be living in fear. Lonely nights and knowing possibly that she could lose her husband to the streets, or to a jail cell; she didn't know if she could handle all of that.

Feeling a bit tipsy from the shots Imani was starting to feel good, the more she drank the more relaxed and loose she became, as the liquor started to fill her system Imani seductively started to swing her hips to the beat slowly, her favorite song was bumpin' through the speakers Don't by Bryson Tiller...

Don't play with her, don't be dishonest .....

Still not understanding this logic.... I'm back & I'm better....

I want you bad as ever....

Adonis was watching her as she swayed to the beat. From across the room, they locked eyes and for a moment it was like they were the only two people in the room. The way she bit her lips as her she rocked from side to side made his dick hard, but he had to hold his composure. It was almost time to let her know everything and that he was finally done with The Dynasty and Derricks bullshit for good. He started to approach her, but before he could Truth had stepped into his path.

"Aye bruh I know you seen I been calling you. Yo pops been talking crazy. Saying you a dead man if you try to leave the squad and..." Truth started before Adonis cut him short.

"And what Truth?" Adonis questioned Truth now had his full attention.

"He said if you don't come meet up with him to figure out what to with all that cocaine sitting in the warehouse he gonna make you pay by making the one thing you love the most disappear."

Truth was only trying to put fear in Adonis heart. Deep down, he knew he was full of shit. Yes, Derrick did say he wanted to speak with his son, but he never said that he would hurt him or kill what he loved which of course would be no one else but Imani. The thought of that made Truths heart sank. He really missed being around Adonis. Being in his presence sent chills down his spine. If he could, he would do anything to have him. That's why he tried to scare him into coming back home where he belonged, running The Dynasty with him and his father. He knew it would be a challenge, but he just had to try. The thought of losing him to Imani killed him on the inside. Adonis could see Imani watching him and Truth from a distance at the opposite side of the club. He could already see that she just knew in her mind that he was gonna make some excuse to ruin their special night by running out to handle one his father's demands.

"Look, whatever my pops tripping about don't mean shit to me anymore. He not that crazy. My decision is final. I have to do better as a man. Being a kingpin for my father' s business isn't gonna be my life. I refuse to lose Imani for anybody or anything! If he wanna send death threats, let him. It's fucked up but at the end of the day I got me. I can look out for myself." Adonis exclaimed.

Looking astonished, Truth was boiling on the inside. He could tell that Adonis meant just what he said and that no matter what lies he told him, he wasn't gonna back down. Not even against his own father.

"Now Truth this ain't no disrespect towards you. I still want us to be cool. You my nigga, my ace, but I need you to respect the fact that this is my choice and that I'm not changing my mind."

Leaving Truth looking lost by the bar, Adonis hugged Imani from behind. "So what was that all about rolling her eyes."

"That's what we need to talk about." Waving his hands at one of the security guards, Adonis led Imani to one of the private rooms of the club. Both of their hearts were beating fast not knowing what to expect from the other. "Babe I've been doing a lot of thinking over the past two years a lot of what you been telling me about The Dynasty, my pops, and just dealing with me as a man. I know for a fact this hasn't been easy. I've made the decision not only for me but for us." Imani's eyes began to water. "I'm not gonna run the business anymore."

As she finally heard the words she had been dying to hear, the tears came flowing from her eyes. She was so overjoyed and excited. She kissed his lips while Imani caressed his face.

"Baby are you for real? Finally, this is all over?"

"Yes I'm done. I know my father is gonna try to do whatever he can to suck me back in that's why Truth really came through tonight. He saying Pops trying to have me hurt or worse."

"What! Baby No!" Imani said panicking.

"Don't worry Imani. If its anyone I know better than I know myself, it's you my beautiful Queen, and Derrick King. He may be crazy, but he not that ruthless. No matter what happens we gonna be good. Don't you ever forget that ma." Adonis reassured her.

"You say that now Adonis and look what happened to Marvin Gaye. His father shot him in cold blood because he was envious and jealous of him. Did Truth even offer to look out for you? Instead of running up in here playing snitch, I bet he told Derrick he was going somewhere else only just to come down here and squeal on him. I know that's your home boy but I don't trust him. Never have and never will. You should trust what I'm telling you bae." Imani pleaded looking into Adonis' eyes.

"Look Truth is more loyal to me than to my old man. He would never go out on some pussy type shit or try to play both sides. He been my nigga for years and I never had to question his loyalty.

****

Secretly in the adjoining room listening through the cracked door, Truth could hear Adonis taking up for him. Smiling to himself, he loved the fact that his crush was taking up for him. He was still pissed. He didn't give two fucks if Imani didn't trust him. He never cared for her ass since the first day they met. She was so stuck up and selfish in his eyes. She wanted to keep Adonis all to herself. When Adonis had been locked up serving time, she tried to get him to cut Truth out of his life then. Sucking his teeth remembering what had happened, he just couldn't help but to think of how stupid and naïve Imani must be. Didn't she know that bros came before hoes? Truth snickered in the cut.

As they embraced, Adonis whispered in Imani's ear, "I promise you from here on out things are gonna be better. Nobody can come between us. Not my father, not Truth, or anyone else that tries to tear us apart." Adonis promised her.

"That's what the fuck you think!' Truth said boastfully not realizing he could be heard.

"Baby did you hear something?" Imani let go of him observing the room.

"No baby it's just me and you in here." Adonis said brushing her off.

Thankful that he hadn't been caught lurking, he continued to mug the happy couple devishly from afar. He could see through that fake ass smile Imani had plastered all over her face. That bitch was scared out of her mind with worry, and she had every right to be. It was no way in the hell Truth was gonna let Imani have his happily ever after. All he had to do was come up with a plan.

"Smile now bitch, but best believe Imma have the last laugh."

Chapter 4

Derrick was at his bachelor pad pissed. Truth had taken over for Adonis since he had chosen to leave, but he didn't trust him fully. He was hoping that threat he had spoken to Truth would make its way back to Adonis. He knew the rules were to never snitch, but he was hoping the nigga would run back and squeal. Shit with Adonis gone, shit had been rough. Not one shipment had been made and the warehouse was stocked with product, which meant The Dynasty was losing money. If there was one thing Derrick King hated to lose out on it was money. The next best thing to new pussy was money to Derrick. To him, it made the world go round.

The one thing that wasn't in Derricks favor was that Adonis had his blood running through his veins. He knew deep down that he wouldn't be easily scared or feel threatened by his words. He didn't raise a punk and for that he knew he was dealing with a tough situation. His son was just as stubborn as him. It was no way Derrick could let Truth be in charge for much longer. He only fucked with him for Adonis' sake. For the past 5 years, he had heard rumors from one of his sources that the nigga was on the DL for the longest and Derrick couldn't stand the thought of it. To him, it was way too many bitches with good pussy to be fucking niggas in the ass. Just the thought of another nigga touching his ass made Derrick squirm in his wheelchair.

Just as he was trying to get the disgusting images out of his head, he heard a knock at the door.

"Who is it?" He questioned. It was late as fuck and he wasn't expecting anybody at this hour.

"It's me Mya, can we talk?"

He became irritated soon as he heard her voice. Mya had been Derricks assistant and fuck buddy for the past two years. At first they would just fuck with each other from time to time, but lately she was getting to be too clingy and becoming heavy on his dick. She was aggravating the fuck out of him saying she had fallen in love with him and what not. The pussy was good, but he couldn't put his all into her. His motto was to never trust these bitches. All these hoes had sneaky motives. For all he knew, Mya could just want him for his money or to try to give one of her side niggas information on his business. He didn't know what her true intentions were, which is why he was trying to cut her ass off with a quickness.

"I know you have a lot going on right now," Mya began, "but I just wanna here for you and help you with whatever you need.'

"Look that's cool and all, but right now I need my space. That shit Adonis pulled was a low blow. It got me all twisted and I gotta figure out what to do next."

"I won't distract you!" Mya interrupted him anxiously. "I just wanna be your medicine." She said taking off her jacket and kneeling herself right in front of Derrick. He wanted to pull away and resist, but the sight of her ripe titties pushed up in her blouse made him hard. He wanted her plump lips to caress and kiss his fat chocolate pole. Pulling it out of his pants, Mya began to lick the head. Starting slow and then building up her rhythm, she began to swallow his whole dick in her mouth.

"Damn, spit on it baby." Derrick moaned heavily. Making sure his dick was coated with her spit she made sure to teabag his balls like they were the best meal she ever had.

If Mya could do nothing else she was a pro at pleasing a man. Giving head was just one of her many specialties. Becoming fast paced with the stroking of her

A BOSS AND HIS RIDER: A CHICAGO LOVE AFFAIR   DOMANEQUE BANKS

tongue, all Derrick could do was squirm and hold on to the back of Mya's head. He didn't wanna look soft, but this bitch could suck the hell out of a dick. Preparing to release his nut on her double-d breast, she placed his throbbing dick in between them both. The hardness of it made him bounce up and down harder.

"OH shit. Fuck!!" Cumming hard, Derrick squirted his cum all over her full breast. Mya jumped up and went to wash off quickly. She knew he didn't like his scent to linger on her after they fucked.

"Did you like that daddy?"

"Yeah I needed that no doubt, but now I need to get back to work. I got an ass of product that hasn't been moved from the warehouse. I'm not trying to get busted by the narcs. Truth hasn't even gotten back with me yet. We need some more workers on the team and not sorry ones. People we can possibly trust to help us move all this shit." Derrick stressed. "Daddy don't worry shit will be good you just gotta get a new headman. Even if you can't get Adonis to come back, you can get my brother. He been wanting to be down with ya'll for the longest!"

All Derrick could do was shake his head. "I knew you was a grimy bitch."

"Excuse me?" Mya asked looking confused.

"Bitch ain't nobody stupid! You think I was born yesterday? I know my son he just strung out over that bitch Imani. He don't mean what he talking about right now. Even if he never did come back I would never give my business over to a stranger, let alone your soft ass brother!"

"It was just a suggestion Derrick. You didn't have to be an asshole about it. Anyways, I don't know why I'm having this conversation with you. You just like all the rest of these trifling hoes. Just looking for a come up out of Chicago. Nice try!"

"I don't know why you just can't let me in?" Mya questioned looking hurt. "We been kicking it for two years. It has to be something you feel for me in your heart. Just tell me what it is? Is it because you can't walk? My age? I have tried to prove my loyalty but you just treat me like I mean nothing to you! I'm human Derrick. My feelings matter!"

Becoming emotional, Mya's eyes filled with tears. The girl was lost. All she wanted to feel was love, and to be accepted by him. If he could just stop putting up this brick wall she just knew that they could have something between them that was real and genuine.

"You need to get out of your feelings ma. A nigga like me can't be with just one female, I could never trust you." He said coldly.

Mya didn't know that Derrick was once married or the fact that Adonis' mother had abandoned them. He didn't want anyone to have sympathy for him. At this time in his life, a relationship wasn't even an option. It was too much money to be made and territories to be built or taken. He had it set in his mind that love was just a four letter word and that it would never cross his lips. The more that she pressured him, the more turned off he was becoming.

"So basically you saying these past two years have meant nothing to you?"

"Look it's been real, but I'm not going through this shit with you. I know that you think you not being a distraction but you are. Lately you been stepping out yo lane wanting more than what I'm able to give you. I think we should just dead it. I'm a grown ass man and I'm never gonna change my mind about not wanting to be with you." Hearing him say those words made Mya's heart drop. She was not only hurt, but angry as hell.

"How dare you use me nigga?" Do you know how

many niggas you fucked with that actually wanted to talk to me and I turned them down all for your crippled ass!" Before she could stop the words they had already flew out of her mouth. She was pissed but never meant to bring up the fact that he couldn't walk.

"Get the fuck out of my house you dumb whore!" Derrick roared.

"I'm sorry!" Mya cried. "I didn't mean it you just made me so fucking mad. You can't you see how much I love you!"

"I'm not gonna tell you again, we done. Now get your raggedy ass and get the hell out my spot. You was just good for busting quick nuts anyway stupid bitch!" Derrick said as spit spewed out his mouth.

Feeling destroyed, Mya picked up her bag and headed for the door. "I am truly sorry Derrick. All I wanted was to be with you."

Closing the door in her face, Derrick rolled himself over to his private bar. He grabbed the Jack Daniels and drank the liquor straight out the bottle. He was so damn pissed. He didn't like the fact that he let Mya destroy his ego by bringing up the fact that he couldn't walk. Ever since he took that bullet 10 years ago, it was a struggle. Losing his ability to walk was one of the worse things that could have happened to him. He and Truth were gonna have to find a way to get Adonis. Desperate times called for desperate measures. At this point, nothing was off limits. Not even his own flesh and blood.

Chapter 5

Since Imani had got wind that Adonis was finally giving up The Dynasty for good, they were making love nonstop. Spending quality time together and for the first time in 5 years, she was starting to feel like she was his number one priority. He didn't propose to her like she and Nyla had initially thought, but she shrugged it off. Imani was just grateful to have her man all to herself again. No more late night calls to run and jump up at any time that Derrick or Truth would call. Since that night at the club, Nyla had kept worrying about what went down that night and today was no different. Nyla and Imani both agreed to meet at Gibson's Bar and Steakhouse to catch up.

"Bitch are you gonna tell me what happened the other night? I see you still ain't got a ring on that finger." Nyla stated pointing out the obvious.

"No he didn't propose. But he did say he was gonna start putting me first before all of his work and making more time for us." I said happily.

Nyla was looking at her crazy, "I thought you said he had some big announcement to make. I know good and well that wasn't it. I would have been mad as hell." Nyla said curling her lip.

"He knew that would mean everything to me. You know he been hella busy lately. The distance and long work nights were killing us." Imani said. She didn't even sound sincere. Imani hated the fact that she was lying to her friend, but she really saw no point in bringing up the fact that Adonis use to sell drugs. Soon, that whole thing would become a phase of the past. "Just know we good now. I'm sure he will pop the question when he is ready Nyla."

"Ya'll been together 5 years. What the hell could he possibly be waiting on?" Nyla questioned.

"Nyla I believe in fate and things happening just at the right time. I know for a fact that Adonis loves me and that's all that matters. He knows not to keep me waiting forever." She said sipping her Mango-Peach Margarita.

"Bitch you hounding me but ummm when you gonna give Troy that baby he wants?" Imani said chuckling. She knew good and well Nyla didn't want any kids.

"Now bitch you being real petty you know I'm not ready for all that. I feel like we need to be way more established before we start having kids. Plus, we still young. I just wanna enjoy it being just us for a while. I wish he could just be okay with that, but girl every time I try to avoid the topic he still presses me about it. Hell I'm starting to think he gonna ask me to marry him after a while." She said laughing out loud.

"So shit what would be so wrong with that?" Imani questioned. "Nyla life is too short. I know you love him to death, and even though it's only been two years for you guys, you still know when it's real."

"True." Nyla sighed. "I just don't want him to think imma become some house wife. If we do decide to get married, bitch I'm calling the shots. Ain't no controlling me no sir!"

Imani couldn't help but to laugh at her. Ny was crazy as hell, but that was just one of the things that she loved about her. As they were just having girls time and enjoying one another's company, Nyla's phone started to ring. Noticing it was Troy's name popping up on her screen, she got all excited. She loved when her boo called just to check up on her.

"Hey Bae." Nyla answered on the 6th ring.

"Where are you? We need to talk." Troy asked sounding like he was about to break down in tears. Nyla could tell something wasn't right.

"Are you ok babe?"

"No baby them mothafuckas killed my Uncle Louis!"

"Wait what?" Nyla questioned. "Your uncle was missing. Oh my God! I can't believe this."

"No we just figured he was away on business as usual, so nobody even assumed he was missing. He was only out for a week." Troy was trying to explain.

"Is everything okay?" Imani asked. She could see the tears welling up in Nyla's eyes from across the table. Nyla was in complete shock. She could hear the words coming out of Troy's mouth, but didn't want to believe they were true.

From the moment that her and Troy started talking, she remembered Troy introducing her to his Uncle Louis. Everyone called him Louie for short. When all of Troy's family members were acting short with her that day, he was the complete opposite. He was always showing her love and cracking jokes. He was such a sweet man, and Troy looked at him as not just an uncle, but as a second father.

"Where did they find him?" Nyla said as the tears were falling over her face.

"Somebody said in a stuffed bag in an abandoned trunk downtown near some music store. The lady had been complaining about a foul smell, so the police came to investigate. I don't know all the details are fuzzy, I really just can't deal with all this right now. I just wanna know who the fuck did this!" Troy was in tears and the rage he had been trying to hold in since he found out the news was finally breaking him.

"Can you come home?" Troy asked wiping his face quickly.

"Baby why would you even ask me that. You know I'm coming right now. Don't worry we gonna get through this together. I love you Troy."

"I love you too Ny." Troy replied hanging up. As

Nyla hung up the phone, she started to sob uncontrollably. It all felt like a bad dream. She hated the fact that her man was hurting.

"Imani, Troy's uncle was found dead. They murdered him. Remember the one we were talking about a couple of months ago?"

"Yes oh my god! I'm so sorry boo." She said handing Nyla some tissues to wipe her face.

"I'm sorry I gotta cut our time short, but Troy really needs me right now." Nyla said standing up gathering her belongings.

"It's ok girl go be with your man. You call me later after everything is settled down. I'll be here and please send Troy me and Adonis's condolences."

"I will. I love you girl."

"I love you too Nyla."

As Nyla left, all Imani could do was feel hurt and upset for her friend. Times like this made her so grateful that Adonis had finally made the choice to leave The Dynasty and the whole city of Chicago alone. She couldn't bare the image of seeing him in a casket dead because of his father's selfishness. Staring outside the window of the restaurant, Imani couldn't help but to believe that the streets held no love for the souls that they took.

Chapter 6

Sitting on the kitchen island, Imani was shaking her head as she read the morning newspaper. She had just finished cooking breakfast for her and Adonis and was flipping through it to see what was going on in the city. Looking at the obituary section, she came across Troy's uncle. He was about Adonis' father's age and had a young wife and two small kids.

"Babe hey here's the picture of Troy's Uncle I was telling you about." Adonis grabbed the paper from Imani. As he looked at the picture, he couldn't believe the image that was staring back at him. His face had looked as if he had just shitted on himself.

"Babe you straight you look like you just seen a ghost." Imani asked.

"Oh naw I'm good I just had something on my mind." He said throwing the paper on the island counter.

He couldn't believe this shit. How could Troy's uncle be his father's partner Louie? Truth and the other men were supposed to have gotten rid of the body so it could never be discovered. Anytime they killed anyone, they had shit on lock. Now that Louie's body had turned up, he knew it wouldn't be long before they started to investigate his mysterious death. Despite him leaving the business, he was gonna have to talk to Truth or his pops to figure out what the fuck was going on. He knew he was gonna have to come up with an excuse to leave the house since he promised Imani they could chill for the day.

He hated to cancel their plans but if he didn't find out what exactly was going on, he could risk himself going to jail for murder or worse.

"Aye babe I'm 'bout to run out real quick and get my car looked at. The brakes been squeaking and shit."

"Okay what time will you be back?" Imani questioned.

"I won't be long, maybe an hour or two at the most." Adonis answered grabbing his car keys and giving Imani a kiss on the lips. "Keep that pussy wet for me." He said playfully as he headed out the door. Imani was laughing at him but she couldn't seem to shake why Adonis got so shook by looking at Troy uncle picture. The shit was odd. Once Adonis got on the road he dialed Truth's number. No answer. That's weird Truth was always by his phone and even though they hadn't been talking really he knew this nigga would always pick despite if they were on good or bad terms. Adonis tried three more times to call Truth, but he didn't answer. He was trying to meet up with this nigga instead of having to go looking for him, or having to pop up at the warehouse. Knowing he was gonna have no choice but to go down there, he felt guilty as hell.

Adonis had made a promise to cut off The Dynasty for good and the fact that he was going down to the warehouse to search for Truth made him feel bad. He didn't wanna get back caught up in his father's shit. Deep down, he truly wanted to change for the better. If Imani even found out any of the recent shit that went down with Troy's uncle he could end up losing her for good.

Pulling into the warehouse parking lot, he automatically spotted Truth's car in the parking lot.

"Really so this nigga was ignoring my phone call." Adonis muttered under his breath.

Entering the warehouse through the back way he called Truths name. He didn't see anyone and all the lights were cut off. It was pitch black. Flipping on the main light, Adonis was shocked by what he discovered. It was an ass of product and guns. He couldn't believe the shit was just lying there out in the open. If the police got a tip from just one snitch on the street, the police would raid the whole place and lock everybody up. Suddenly he heard a noise coming from the back office. Not sure of what it was, Adonis pulled his gun out in case he had to pop a nigga off. If somebody was in this motherfucker with all the lights off, it had to be a thief. If he saw them he was gonna shoot his ass. Kicking the door down and flipping the light on, he saw Truth had Mya bent over his pops desk fucking her straight in the ass. They both jumped from the loud noise looking shocked.

"Omg!" Mya screamed as she tried to hurry up and find her dress she had on earlier.

"The fuck kind of shit ya'll got going on?" Adonis questioned. He knew that Mya wasn't in a relationship with his pops, but she still fucked with him heavily. He thought she would have enough respect not to fuck one of his workers, and on his desk for that matter.

"Nigga I been calling you. We need to talk now. Can you put on some clothes? I don't wanna see all your privates and shit.

Truth was mad as fuck. He was hoping that Adonis would at least sneak and try to catch a quick glance at his dick. He really didn't mean to get caught up with Mya, she had come to the warehouse looking for Derrick and was crying to him about how he had cut her off. Truth was still dealing with the fact that he no longer had his ace by his side. No matter how hard he tried, he knew he couldn't move weight like Adonis. When it was both of them together they made a great team.

"You was so busy getting pussy that you ignored my phone call?" Adonis questioned.

"Nigga don't try to come in here checking me about shit." Truth replied. "I been having to bust my ass to make up for the shit you left us with, and despite what the fuck you say I don't have to run and jump when you call me. You made it seem like we wasn't cool after you just abandoned everybody to go legit. You said fuck the Dynasty and our friendship."

"Man stop acting like a bitch. I told you already, you still my boy regardless of the fact. I just didn't want to be caught up in anymore of my pops bullshit." Adonis replied shaking his head.

"So why you over here?" I mean you said you was done with it so why you snoopin back around?" Truth asked putting on a front. He was secretly hoping that Adonis had finally come to his senses and changed his mind. He missed everything about this man. From the sound of his voice, to the cologne that he wore every day, not having his man by his side was tearing him up mentally.

"You know why I'm here, and Mya I think you may wanna leave before my pops gets back. I don't wanna have to explain this bullshit to him." Adonis spoke dryly.

"Look Adonis please don't make me go. I know this doesn't look right, but it's not what it looks like." Mya continued. "Your father cut me off after a big misunderstanding between the two of us. I only came here to make piece and see him. Truth just happened to be here and we just had a moment." Mya pleaded.

"Don't flatter yourself ma. You came in here jumping all on my dick." Truth interrupted her. How dare she have the nerve to say they had a moment in front of his future husband. This bitch was being over dramatic. Hoping that she would just leave, he continued to make his point clear to her and Adonis.

"Look I won't mention this if you don't. I mean it happened, it was a mistake, and it won't be happening again." Truth stated. He wanted so much to feel bad about what happened between him and Mya, but why when Adonis just up and fucked him over.

"I think the best thing for you to do is go." Adonis

told Mya. "This is already messed up enough, and truth be told I'm not trying to run into my pops. I'm just here to speak to Truth."

"You know what forget it?" Mya sucked her teeth. "I'll try to get in touch with him later. Truth you better not tell Derrick anything about what happened today. I know you both think I'm not shit because of what we just did Truth, but regardless of what you two may think of me I love your father Adonis. I will not just throw away what we have over a simple misunderstanding." And with that Mya had left out the back door.

"Really Truth? So out of all the bitches you can fuck you wanna jump on my pops assistant?"

"Man fuck all that. You ain't been worried about your pops or nobody else since the day you walked out on everybody for your own selfish reasons. Now you wanna bust up in here like you give a fuck thinking we good. What you even doing down here? As you can see we got enough shit on our hands as it is. This cocaine and weed been sitting here for weeks. We only have 7 men to push everything we got, and your father don't trust any of them." Truth ranted.

"Man ya'll worried about pushing product when we got bigger shit worry about! Nigga have you not been listening to the news or the streets? Louie body been discovered by the cops. Now how the fuck that happen Truth!?"

Looking shocked and freaked out at the same time Truth was honestly at a loss for words. He had no idea that Louie body had turned up. He hadn't even heard about anything because he was too busy trying to deal with getting rid of all of that product that they had.

"That can't be true. We drove outta state to get rid of Louie body for special reasons. Ain't no way that body could have turned up unless somebody personally dug it up for it to be found." Truth said searching for his phone.

"So explain this shit then?" Adonis replied throwing the newspaper article in front of him. Truth read the article and couldn't believe what he was reading. The police had found Louie's body in front of the music store downtown. The picture of the car in the article wasn't the one they dumped in the water with Louie's body.

"I swear bro on everything some shit just ain't adding up. We dumped Louie body in one of the cars parked behind the warehouse. That shit they found his body in look brand new. I know I done made my fair share of mistakes the last couple of weeks, but I would never be so messy to where the cops could trail us to a dead body." Truth stated looking Adonis straight in the eyes. Adonis ain't know what the hell to believe anymore. He knew if this shit got back to Imani that he was responsible for killing Troy's uncle, she would never be able to forgive him.

"Look we gotta find out who the fuck left that body there man. Imani home girl boyfriend is Louie's nephew. If she found out I killed him she won't be able to look at me the same. So we gonna have to figure this shit out." Adonis demanded.

"That's the only reason you came down here cuz. You trying to cover this shit up before Imani finds out. You need to be worried about all of us taking the fall for this shit. The same mothafucka who has been stealing from us is probably the same person who set this whole charade down. Here you are worried about that bitch when we need to be focused on not going to prison for life for murder!!" He screamed at Adonis.

"Nigga who the fuck you yelling at!" Adonis said pulling out his gun. Truth was speechless. In the 8 years he knew Adonis, he never expected for him to pull out a gun on him. "Now let me get something straight you. Imma tell you ass for the last time, my wife ain't no bitch. When you talk to me you need to lose that bass out ya tone! I'll be damn if I let you keep chumping me off!" Adonis roared. He was mad as hell.

The very thing he was trying to leave out of his life was coming back to haunt him in the worst way. If the cops found out he was the one who pulled the trigger, he knew he would be gone for life, especially with all the previous charges he had on him from the last time. He couldn't imagine spending the rest of his life without Imani. She was his world and without her, his world had no light.

"Now my pops probably done seen this shit in the paper already. He gonna be wondering why the fuck you ain't cover your tracks, that's if he don't try to kill you first. So we gotta work together to get down to the bottom of this. I ain't going down for no more of this shit and for your mistakes." Adonis said still pointing the gun at Truth.

Truth had tears in eyes. The man that he had fallen in love with had a gun pointed ready to kill him. "You are so selfish"" Truth said as the tears slipped down his cheek. "You can't even realize when you have a good thing staring you right in the face."

Adonis was still looking lost. "The fuck are you talking about?" Adonis asked looking at him strangely. Truth was acting like a punk crying and shit. All he was trying to do was get his point across. If a nigga felt like his woman or his freedom was at risk, Adonis was gonna die trying to protect.

Truth wanted to tell Adonis how he truly felt, but was scared of how he might react. He already had a gun in his hand and he didn't want to get shot.

"Can you just chill out bruh? Look I'm sorry. I ain't mean what I said. You just getting all out of shape about Louie and you freaking me out. I wanna know who set this shit up as much as you do." Truth said. Lowering his gun, Adonis decided to chill out. He was already pissed and really didn't wanna have to shoot Truth. Over the years, he gave him consistent loyalty and that was the only reason why he truly fucked with him to begin with.

"I know I don't have a solid plan, but just give me a day or two to figure something out. I'll get out in the streets. Somebody gonna be bound to know something." Truth continued.

"Alright nigga you got 24 hours to get something, and I mean it. When you find out something hit my line. Same number ain't shit changed."

"Ok cool I'll hit you back." Truth said. Adonis put his gun back in his strap and started to walk off.

"Remember what I said 24 hours and don't tell my father you seen me either." Adonis stated firmly.

"Man you got my word." Truth replied. Truth had just enough time to try at least find out the truth of how Louie's body had turned up back in Chicago. If he didn't, not only could he possibly get killed, but Adonis could go to jail and he could do time for accessory to murder. He just knew if he could get Imani out of the way that Adonis could see that he didn't need her for anything. With him, he would always be protected and looked out for. If he could possibly figure out who had sat them up maybe Adonis would see him in a new light. Glancing at his watch, he saw it was going on 7pm. He had until tomorrow night to get his plan together,and he planned on wasting no more time.

Chapter 7

Imani was waiting for Adonis to return home from getting his car fixed or looked at. He said he would be back an hour ago, but by now 4 hours had passed and still no sign of him. No phone call or text to explain where he was or why he was so late. She had been calling his phone over and over, and each time it went straight to voicemail. The more time passed, the more she wondered where the fuck he could possibly be. Hearing her phone ring, she jumped up thinking that it was him calling. Looking at the screen she noticed that it was a blocked number.

"Hello," she answered. Silence. "Hello who is this?" She questioned then a dial tone. "Motherfuckers love playing on the phone." She said herself. She didn't have time for the games tonight. She was already highly pissed because her day hadn't gone as planned. Just as she about to dial his line again, she heard keys turning in the front door.

"Baby I can explain." Adonis said as he stepped foot in the house.

"Nigga you said you would be home more than 4 hours ago!!! You know how long I been trying to call you?" She screamed.

"I'm sorry man my phone died. I went to get the car looked up and the guy at the shop ended up fixing it. Can you chill? You act like its late at night or some shit!" He yelled back.

Imani could tell all over his face that he was lying and the more he tried to play it off, the more pissed she was becoming.

"Adonis if you were at the auto place, why you didn't just call me from the shop to at least let me know you would be okay? Or use somebody else phone? You really must take me for some kind of fool!" she said rolling her eyes.

Adonis hated having to lie to her about what was going on. He couldn't tell her that he was responsible for killing Troy's Uncle. She would never understand why he did it. If he even told her why he was working with Truth she would think he was backing out of leaving The Dynasty. He knew they were all in some deep shit and the fact that he couldn't vent to the one person he trusted the most really messed with his head. Whoever had sat them up wanted him to go down for Louie's death or else why would they go through the trouble of pulling the car his body was dumped in and bring it all the way back to Chicago. It was too much work and only a smart motherfucker could pull it off. Lost in thought, Imani was snapping to get his attention.

"Nigga have you heard anything I said?" She asked him for the 5th time.

"Yo ma chill ain't nobody lying to you". He said attempting to hold her wrist. Pulling away she leaned up against the kitchen counter folding her arms together.

"Just tell me who you fucking Adonis?"

"Wait so that's where you think I've been? You think I been out with a bitch? Damn a nigga can't even go get his car fixed without you jumping to all these crazy all conclusions!"

"No because you know what Adonis, I know you like the back of my hand. Ain't no way that you were gone getting your car fixed and you always take your portable charger with you to avoid it dying, so don't try to play me! I hope you had fun with your little whore!" She said attempting to swing at him.

"Imani chill the fuck out!" He said throwing her hands up against the wall.

"Let me go!!" She screamed becoming more irritated. "I been with you for too long for you to lie to me like I'm some dumb young girl who's so thirsty to be with you that I'll accept any lie that you throw my way. I won't put up any bullshit from you or any other man!"

"Imani I would never cheat on you and you know that. Why can't you just trust me ma!?"

"Look I'm sorry but bae I know when something is off with you. If it's not a female it has to be something. You left here early this afternoon like a bat out of hell after we had our day planned. Then you make up some bullshit excuse about your phone being dead. It doesn't make sense. I want the truth."

"Sometimes the truth ain't what you wanna hear." He retorted back.

Looking uneasy Imani sat down on the edge of their king size bed. "Ok now you starting to scare me Adonis. Tell me what the hell is going on now."

"It ain't nothing like that but Truth is caught up in some deep shit Imani, and I gotta help him. I kind of caused it to begin with." Adonis partially confessed.

"What you mean kind of? You promised me that you would stay out of your fathers and Truth's fuckery. For a month now you been telling me this shit is a wrap and that we can finally live our lives without worrying about what the fuck they have going on. You told me you were done! Damn! So you been playing me this whole time?" She said shaking her head. "I knew you wouldn't be able to do it."

Adonis was growing more frustrated the more he tried to explain himself. "You knew this shit wasn't gonna be easy to break away from. I'm busting my ass trying to prove to you that I'm a changed man. I'm doing my best to trade all this bullshit for you! For us!" Adonis roared. "You questioning my love for you, my faithfulness to you and my loyalty! Since we been together, I haven't even touched or thought about fucking another female. I never even gave you a reason to think that so why even come at me sideways about it?" Adonis said checking her.

Imani stood in silence. She never meant to question Adonis' loyalty or come off insecure, but she just couldn't help herself. "I'm just scared." She said, "I don't wanna lose you Adonis. You have always been able to be honest with me, and now I'm just worried that what you doing with Truth will get you back locked up or worse." She said trying to hold back her tears.

"Come here." he demanded. Looking down towards the floor he quickly tilted her head up and kissed her deeply.

"Baby I'm Sorry." She tried to explain.

"Shhhhhhh don't talk." Picking her up by her waist, he laid her down on the bed. He pushed her dress up above her waist and started to taste her honey pot.

"Ooooohh," she moaned softly. "Baby you feel so good." Imani was so confused in that moment. She was in bliss, but her heart really hurt on the inside. She wanted to be able to enjoy the trembles and pleasure that came from her insides, but she felt so scared for Adonis. As she closed her eyes to treasure the moment, she started to dream of the future that they would have. Images of their wedding, her birthing his seed, them lying in each-others arms all filled her mind.

"Baby you taste so good damn I love you." Adonis spoke between licking her fat pussy lips. Imani couldn't control the ecstasy that was about to emerge from her body. Her thoughts quickly changed to seeing Adonis behind the bars of a prison cell, seeing him in a coffin, and her and the kids they shared visiting his grave clouded her thoughts as she finally exploded in pleasure. The tears rolled down her cheeks.

"Why you crying?" Adonis asked trying to hold her, but she pulled away. I just wanna go to sleep babe. She turned over facing her back towards him. Laying down beside her facing his back towards her own, Adonis knew he had to fix this shit. The last thing he wanted to do was keep secrets from Imani, but he knew he had to protect her heart. Coming clean would only make shit worse.

Just as he was about to fall asleep his cellphone started to ring. Looking at the dialer he saw it was Truth calling. Getting up to go downstairs to take the call, he picked up the phone.

"Aye I think I got something." Truth stated without even bothering to say hello.

"You think or you know." Adonis said.

"Look can you just meet me at my crib around 11."

"Why can't we just meet now. Imani sleeping so you need to make this fast so I can hurry and get back." Adonis said getting agitated.

Rolling his eyes, Truth sucked his teeth. Shit he needed more time before he could get his plan together. "Can you at least give me another hour?" Truth asked praying he said yes.

"Yeah 1 hour." Adonis said as he hung up. He knew Adonis was still pissed because someone was after them, but that didn't mean he had to hang up in his face. Smiling to himself, he quickly shook it off. "Bae is just cranky." He said to himself. "By the end of tonight he will good and satisfied."

One hour was just enough time for Truth to put his whole plan together. He had no real leads in finding out the truth in what was going on, but by this time tomorrow he would. He just needed to get Adonis alone so he could try to get through to him in his own special way.

Walking back into the room, Adonis saw Imani

was knocked out. He decided to leave her a note on her coffee stand to let her know he would be out for a minute. Praying that things would be better by the end of the week, all Adonis could do was hope for the best. No matter how many obstacles they had faced in the past, him and Imani overcame it all. Now he was hoping more than ever that they could overcome this trial.

Chapter 8

Troy was down at the local pub having a drink. Ever since the death of his uncle, he felt lost. Nyla had been doing her best to try to help him cope with the lost, but he just kept pushing her away. He had been hearing all type of shit in the streets about how a nigga named Derrick King murdered his uncle and Troy wanted nothing but revenge. Troy wasn't the type of nigga to just snap and kill somebody. He wasn't built for it. The anger and the rage he felt for his Uncle was something he just couldn't deal with or bare. It wasn't fair that his life was ripped from him, that his kids would have to now live without a father and that his aunt would now have to live without a husband.

Calling the bartender back over he asked her for another round of whiskey. His phone had been blowing up with messages from Nyla, his mother and some of his friends, but he didn't feel like being bothered right now. He needed to clear his head and find the motherfucker who killed his uncle in cold blood. Sipping on his drink, he noticed a fine woman sitting at the bar a couple of seats over. Trying not to think with his dick and think with his head, he tried not to go over and speak to the milf at the bar. Not only was he drunk, but he was feenin for some pussy. Nyla hadn't been giving him any pussy because she didn't wanna get on birth control and kept saying she had a yeast infection. What yeast infection lasted for three weeks? He knew she was just lying because she didn't want him to cum inside of her. Taking his next drink to the head, he decided to go talk to the older lady at the other side of the bar. Shit, she was sexy as hell. He figured since he was getting satisfied at home he might as well get it from somewhere else.

The lady at the bar had shoulder length black hair and almond skin. She had on a sexy black dress and knee high boots. Her skin looked silkier than a motherfucker. Even though she didn't look older, Troy could tell she was by the way she carried herself. Rocking her shades, she sat at the bar alone seemingly checking out her surroundings.

"How you doing?" Troy asked sitting down beside her.

"Who wants to know?" She said taking off her shades.

Damn she was gorgeous. Her eyes were full and brown. She reminded him of a younger version of Diahann Carroll.

"Maybe I do." He replied curiously. Troy wasn't in his right state of mind. He wasn't thinking of the consequences. The only thing he wanted to take out his were his aggressions. Fuck this woman and worry about his problems later. Tonight he just wanted to have a good time.

"What you doing in a place like this?" He questioned her.

"Can't a woman come back to the city and enjoy herself?"

"Come back? You from here?" Troy questioned.

"Yes I haven't been here in 24 years. I had to go missing in action for a while but now I'm here to tie up some loose ends and reclaim what's mine."

Studying her as she talked he couldn't help but feel intrigued he couldn't help but to want to know more about her. "Sounds like you came back to the city to take care of business." Troy said eyeing her thighs seductively.

"You like what you see." She noticed him looking her over.

"Hell yeah I do." He said playing along with her. "All this cat and mouse we doing can I at least know your name?"

Looking him over, the chocolate cutie had sparked her interest. Coming back to Chicago she knew she was strictly on business, and wanted to keep a low profile.

Not wanting to tell him her real name she decided to lie at least for now. Who knows after a night of fun she may never see him again. She could tell he was drunk. It was all in his eyes, and after not having some good dick in a while, she needed to be man handled by a young buck. The drinks had her pussy throbbing.

"My name is Melissa and what's yours?"

"Troy. What you got planned for the rest of the evening?" He asked downing his last shot.

'Nothing much just gonna go back to my hotel room and drink some more. Would you like to join me?" She asked wondering if he was gonna say yes. She noticed his phone kept ringing off the hook, and he would deny the call every time. As it started to ring again, he put his phone on silent.

"Damn somebody must be ready for you to come home. They keeping a tab on you." She said trying to be nosy.

"Naw I'm good but if the offer still stands I would love to enjoy your company."

"Okay how you about you follow me." She said as she left a $200-dollar tab to cover both her and his tab at the bar. He liked her style already. Stumbling as he walked, she took his car keys from him.

"You leave your car here. You can ride with me tonight." She demanded. The last thing she needed was for him to wreck somewhere and she would feel guilty for something else that she had done wrong in her life. Troy let her take the lead. He didn't care as long as he was in her guts by the end of the night.

Getting in the car, they rode all the way to the

Hilton Hotel in Chicago. He could tell she wasn't no young dumb chick and that she enjoyed the finer things in life. Not wanting to waste another minute, as soon as the elevator doors shut he pushed her up against the wall and fingered her pussy. He was delighted to see she had no panties on. As he finger-fucked her, she became even more turned on. She drowned his fingers with her wetness. She wanted to fuck him right then and there, but she knew they were about to reach her room soon. Pushing him off she bit her bottom lip.

"Slow down young buck, mama gonna let you get it all tonight." She said as they reached her floor to the room.

Seeing Nyla was calling his phone again, he decided to go ahead and answer it just in case it was an emergency.   "Aye let me take this Melissa?" He said stepping into the bathroom.

"Ok you handle your business." She said as she started to undress out of her clothes.

"Yes..." Troy answered the phone sounding dry.

"Nigga have you not seen me calling you?" Nyla said mad as hell. "I'm calling to check on your ass and you wanna ignore my fucking phone calls!?" Nyla knew that he was having a difficult time dealing with his uncle's death, but he had seriously been tripping lately. All he wanted to was go out, get drunk and try to fuck her raw so he could get her pregnant! Something she tried to constantly tell him that she just wasn't ready for.

"Where are you?" She asked him ready to fuck him up.

"Man I'm out with my niggas drinking. You blowing up my phone nagging and shit is messing up my night." Hanging up the phone in her face, he made sure to turn it off so she couldn't keep blowing up his phone with the bullshit. He knew he was being cruel, but shit he was dealing with a lot right now and Nyla was just being a headache. He loved her, but it just seemed like they both wanted different things or as if they were growing apart. Whatever it was, he didn't wanna stress about it tonight. Stepping out the bathroom, he saw Melissa ain't waste no time. She was laying on the bed but ass naked. Her body was shaped like a goddess. Every inch and curve was in the right place. He knew how wet she could get, but now he wanted to taste it. Putting her legs across his shoulders, he started to devour her pussy with his tongue. Her pussy tasted so good in his mouth. He didn't know if it was the liquor or her flavor but she was just for him.

Melissa wanted it rough. It had been months since she had some good dick. This young buck was turning her out and making her speak in tongues. Shoving his face in her pussy, she told him to lick all over her clit.

"Man fuck this shit bend over". He commanded. Flipping over on all fours, he entered her slowly at first. "Damn this shit so fucking tight." He said trying not to bust so fast.

"You like that pussy don't you?" She asked as she started to throw her fat ass on his dick.

"Fuck!" he roared. Troy loved the fact that Melissa was older. Her pussy was fat and juicy and she knew how to work it just right. Shit Nyla was so stiff in bed, and here Melissa was fucking him better than any young bitch could.

"Daddy let me ride you!" She demanded. "Let me ease your mind." Jumping on his dick, she rode him like a black stallion. She loved the way his big curved dick stood up just right inside of her. The more she bounced on it, the better it hit her g-spot.

"You gonna let me nut in that mouth?" Troy questioned. His dick was throbbing inside her. He wanted to bust all over her face and her mouth. "Shit baby I'm 'bout to cum!" Jumping off him, Troy demanded she get down on her knees. Within minutes, he had busted all over her face.

"That was good huh?" She questioned wiping off her face and laying down in the bed.

"It was more than good. You got a nigga all sprung and shit." He said as he laid down in the bed beside her. The room was starting to spin and all he wanted to do was get some rest. Before Troy knew it, it was 6 am and the night's events were all coming back to him as a blur, along with a pounding headache. Looking over to his left side, he saw a beautiful older woman lying beside him naked. "Damn." He said instantly regretting cheating on Nyla. He knew he was in a messed up mindset if he went this far as to cheat on his girl. Deciding not to wake Melissa up, he crept out the bed to find his car keys.

On the night stand, he saw his keys sticking outside of Melissa's purse. He also saw a folded up piece of paper that looked like a newspaper article folded inside of her purse. Opening it up, he saw the article of his uncle Louie's body being found along with his obituary inside and a picture of a dark skin man attached to it. Turning the photo around to see if a name was attached to the picture, he saw the name Derrick King written on the back. Furious, Troy ripped the covers off of Melissa's body!

"Bitch what type of game you playing and how do you know my Uncle?!" Troy yelled ready to beat somebody ass.

"What the hell are you talking about?" Melissa said dazed and confused.

"This is what the fuck I'm talking about!" Troy threw the picture and article at Melissa as she laid down on the bed.

"Why the fuck were you even in my purse to begin with?" She questioned him ready to call the police.

"That should be the least of your worries right now. You got five minutes to explain how the hell you know my Uncle and his killer!"

"Why should I explain anything to you?" Melissa questioned him.

"Because that man was more to me than just a family member. He was not only my uncle, but a second father to me."

Melissa could tell by the sadness in his voice that she owed him some sort of explanation. "The reason I have the article is because I'm just as hurt as you are. Your uncle was my friend from back in the day and his killer was..." She said hesitantly. "Look.... I lied to you last night. My name isn't Melissa..."

"Then what is your real name?" Troy asked confused.

"My real name is Ivy King. Derrick King is my husband."

Chapter 9

Adonis pulled into Truths driveway anxious to hear good news. He just wanted to know what the fuck was really going on. Before coming to Truths place, he stopped by a few of the territories that he used to run to see if he could find out any answers. Everyone was spooked, whoever had tried to come against the Kings was a heavy hitter, and no one wanted to come against them or snitch.

Knocking on Truth's door, he waited for him to come answer. "What up bro?" Adonis walked in & sat on the couch. "So what did you find out?" He questioned getting straight to the topic at hand. Adonis ain't have all night to be fooling around with Truth. Him and Imani were already in a bad state and he didn't wanna make shit worse by staying out all late and having to tell more lies.

"First I did some digging man, and I think I know who been setting all this shit up. I know its gonna sound crazy but after speaking to one of our former associates everything they were telling me it makes perfect sense." Truth was going on and on.

"Man can you just cut the shit and stop talking in circles."

"Alright well word on the street is there is a lady named Ivy from a new territory in New York that has come to get revenge on your father."

"Ok what does that have to do with Louie?"

"Well it seems the lady was a close friend of Louie's from when your pops was young. Her name is Ivy King. They saying it's your mama bruh." Truth revealed.

"Naw you bugging man. Ain't no way. Look I have never met my mother. You know she left me and my pops when I was small. Why would she just show up out the blue after all these years?!" Adonis said feeling confused and upset.

If what he was hearing was true, then his mother was here in Chicago. He wasn't sure how to feel about that. His momma had been gone his whole life, and had missed so many important events and moments. Yes, his father had been there but there was just something's that he wished that he had his momma there to console and comfort him for. Especially since his father didn't really believe in showing emotions. He often still laid awake at night dreaming of what his mother was like and wondering what type of person she was. That feeling never left his heart and the fact that he never met her left an empty piece missing out of Adonis's soul.

"So how we gonna find out if this is even true bro?"

If your mother is really back in the Chi- Town, it won't be hard to track her. Even if she is using another alias, you got so many power connects and so much weight in these streets that somebody will be bound to let you know if it's really her." Truth replied. He was so happy on the inside to be the one to give him this kind of news.

Truth knew just how much he still longed for a relationship with his mother. The fact that Imani couldn't be one to give him such news made him be filled with joy on the inside. He had one up against that wack ass bitch. She just didn't know that he wasn't the one to be fucked with. It was no way in hell he was just gonna let her have Adonis all for himself, and tonight hopefully he could finally make him realize just that.

Pulling out his phone Adonis wanted to call Imani. He knew she would at least be happy to know that his mother could potentially be in town. If anyone knew how much it bothered him to not have his mother in his life it was Imani. On the nights that he lied awake at night with so many questions on his mind, she was the one that was there to hold him and wipe his tears. Imani was the first woman to give him that love that he craved for since he was a child. He had to let the woman he loved know the news. Even if it led him to finding out something negative in the end, it would still be worth the wait.

"Who you calling man?" Truth asked.

"Nigga I'm 'bout to call Imani and tell her the good news. Do you know what this means man? I could be meeting my mom dukes and I want my lady to know bro chill out." Adonis said about to dial Imani's number.

"I can't let you do that bro." Truth said coldly.

"Nigga what the fuck is you talking about?" Adonis replied ready to chump him off, but before he could turn around his world had turned black.

Truth knew the only way to get through to Adonis was if he couldn't leave.

"Thank you for helping me you can leave now after we get him up the stairs."

Mya was looking at Truth like he was crazy. "Look you really got shit twisted if you think I'm leaving here without what you promised me. I held up my end of the deal so now where is my cut?" Mya questioned. He really had her fucked up if she thought she was gonna just help him kidnap his gay crush and not give her any money for it. Mya was already pissed after attempting to get in contact with Derrick after their falling out, and having to come to terms with the fact that he had completely cut her off. He truly didn't really give a fuck about her. She tried to go to his condo to check up on him only to be escorted off the premises by security. After her accidental hook up with Truth, she didn't expect for him to reach out to her for help but he did. They had met for coffee at one of Chicago's famous diners. He confessed to being in love with Adonis and Mya felt a warm spot for him. She knew how he felt because she felt the exact same way about Derrick.

Now that she knew that he honestly didn't give two

fucks about her, she planned to get what was rightfully hers and get the hell out of town. If his crippled ass couldn't value what was already in his face, then that was his lost.

"Look I don't have time for the game I need my money tonight. My flight leaves at 11. If me and my brother gonna make it in time I gotta jet now. I don't have time to help you play cat and mouse with Adonis. You better hope this works out in your favor because he will wake up and kill your ass for tying him up." Mya said looking at him like he was crazy. Truth was acting like a sick in love puppy. So desperate and stupid. Did he honestly think that Adonis would really give up everything just to be with him?

"Bitch imma pay you just help me bring him upstairs."

"Alright damn." Struggling to pull his dead weight up the stairs, they got Adonis in the bed and tied him up tightly. Truth knew that Mya was gonna leave and he didn't wanna take the chance of Adonis waking back up and getting lose. He knew if he could get free, he was gonna be a dead man walking.

"Thank you Ms. Lady." Truth replied happier than a school girl on Christmas day. He quickly pulled out the 20 bands he promised her.

"Where did you get all this money from?" She questioned. She knew Derrick paid him for helping him, but not enough for him to just throw away 20 bands for bullshit.

"Bitch don't worry about it just take your cut and be happy." Truth replied getting smart back at her. Mya had her own suspicions on where the money came from. Not wanting to stir up any drama, she happily took her cut and left out the door. Leaving Chicago was the only way to deal with her broken heart. Plus, she didn't want to be here for the backlash that would come from all this. Starting up her charger, she sped off into the night to catch her plane, promising to never look back.

Chapter 10

Nyla was at Imani's house crying her eyes out. They were both in despair and hurting. After Adonis hadn't returned home last night, she was worried sick. He hadn't answered his phone or cell and Imani wasn't even mad. More than anything, she just wanted her man to come home so they could work things out. After trying to call and text his phone all night, she called the local police department only for them to tell her it had to be more than 72 hours before you can report someone over the age of 18 missing. Nyla knew nothing was wrong with Troy. She knew he didn't want to be with her anymore and now that she needed him more than ever when shit was going south, he had just said fuck everything like the last couple of years meant nothing. Even worse, she was feeling sick and had been throwing up for the past week and a half. Praying she wasn't pregnant, she kept telling herself that her period would show and that it was just late due to stress and aggravation. Using the I-Phone 6 app on her phone, Nyla was able to track Troy. She already knew he had been to a hotel room with a bitch. When she arrived there, she heard the moans and the two of them fucking from outside. Nyla didn't even wanna give him the power to show out, she was done with his ass. She knew losing his uncle would hurt him, but lately he had been treating her like pure shit and making her feel like she was the blame for all of his problems.

Yes, she had been holding off on giving him the pussy because Troy was refusing to use condoms because he wanted a baby with her so bad. The last thing she wanted to feel was trapped. Although she was hurting all she wanted to do at this point was help Imani find Adonis. Shit somebody had to save their relationship even if it wasn't her own.

"Imani, in the letter it said that Adonis was gonna be with Truth right? She asked. As if a lightbulb had gone off in her head, she reread Adonis' letter. It did say he would be with Truth. Knowing she had the niggas number, she also remembered where he lived.

"I need to go to Truth's house." Imani stated. In her heart she knew something wasn't right. She knew after the big ass argument that her and Adonis had that he would never fuck up twice. Her woman's intuition led her to believe that something was really wrong.

"Girl we both going to Truth house. Ain't no way in hell I'm letting you face that nigga alone. You know he ain't got 'em all." Nyla assured Imani. She been peeped something was off about that nigga.

"Okay cool let me throw on my sneakers." Imani was gonna find out what happened to her man she couldn't get that gut feeling out of her system. As they were locking the door of the house, Troy's car pulled up into the driveway.

"Just get in the car Nyla don't event stunt his ass." Imani warned her friend. Shit she was trying to hurry up and go she didn't have time for Troy's shenanigans. Getting into the car Nyla hurried up and locked her door.

"Yo open up we need to talk!" Troy demanded.

"Nigga fuck you I'm done with your cheating ass! I know you was fucking that bitch last night at the Hilton!" Nyla screamed out the window as her and Imani pulled off.

"I can't believe that nigga got the nerve to come looking for you at my house after the way he showed his ass last night." Imani smirked.

Imani was grateful that Adonis never cheated on her in the five years they had been together. She tripped like he would when he would stay out late, but deep down in her heart she knew that her man was faithful. That's why she had to find him so they can fix their issues. They had come too far to let it all go. For Truths own sake, he had better not gotten Adonis caught up in his shit or else that nigga would pay with his life. She knew that as soon as Adonis tried to save him he would get him caught up in his bullshit just like his selfish ass daddy. Pulling onto Truth's street, Imani immediately spotted Truth and Adonis' car in the driveway. Jumping out the car she started banging on the door only for her knocks to be unanswered.

"They gotta be in there." she muttered underneath her breath.

"Bitch wait up." Nyla replied coming up behind her. "You move fast as hell. You gonna have to slow down. I told you I don't want you going to greet this nigga by yourself he crazy!" Nyla yelled at her friend.

"If you think he crazy you ain't seen nothing yet. Now come on! He ain't answering and I know Adonis in here! We gonna have to see if the back door is open or break in." Imani explained heading towards the back of the condo. Climbing over the fence, Imani spotted the back door to the condo. Turning the knob, she realized the door was locked! "Fuck!", She said instantly becoming irritated.

"Look!" Nyla pointed at the tiny mailbox up besides the door. "Check to see what's in it." Nyla replied Checking the box inside was a key. "Jackpot bitch!" Imani said anxiously trying to get inside.

"Alright make sure you open the door so that no one can hear us come in." Nyla warned her friend. She had agreed to come help, but she didn't feel like dying today. Imani was scared to go inside but she had to make sure Adonis was okay. "Ok we gonna move inside and I want you stay behind and watch my back. Here, do you know how use this?" Imani said handing Nyla a handgun out of her purse.

"Damn girl I ain't know you carried a gun!" Nyla said shocked as hell.

"Yes girl I ain't stupid. I have one for me too. Now you gonna be my back up, and if you see anybody try to attack anyone of us, you just pull it out and aim it at them. Don't shoot unless I tell you to." Imani told Nyla.

"I don't know Mani. I never shot anybody before." She said nervously.

"Just chill you got this! I trust you!" Imani reassured her. Using the key to unlock the door, Imani and Nyla entered the back door each holding on tightly to their guns. They noticed all the lights were off downstairs. The only way they could move around and see was from the daylight outside. Even though Truth wasn't shit, Imani had to admit he kept a nice ass place. Everything was neat and clean and designed to a tee. You would honestly think a bitch was living there. Heading towards the stairs, they heard a noise and saw all the lights were on.

"What the fuck is that?" Nyla whispered scared as hell. She was ready to say fuck everything and leave Imani by herself. She was scared out of her mind.

"Girl I don't know!" Imani whispered back. "Have your gun out and stay behind me."

"Okay just come on so we can get this over with!" Nyla hissed back.

Tip Toeing up the stairs, they both checked their surroundings to make sure nobody was upstairs with them. As they reached the bedroom, the noise they heard became louder. Opening the door, Imani couldn't believe her eyes. Adonis was in the bed with nothing but his boxers on, and his legs and wrist were tied to the bed. His mouth was tied up but he was screaming for someone to help him.

"Omg baby! Nyla help me untie him!" Imani screamed. Putting their guns at the foot of the bed, they both scrambled to untie Adonis. Nyla took the legs while Imani got his wrist loose and untied the rope from inside his mouth!

"Omg baby what happened to you?" Imani questioned him while frantically looking over his body to make sure he was ok and not hurt.

"Look bae Truth is crazy! When I see that nigga he is a dead man!"

"Now baby is that any way to talk about your future hubby?!" Truth replied with a crazy look in his eyes. He and Imani were staring each other up and down. The two people who hated each other the most were now face to face. "This sick twisted nigga is gay," Imani thought to herself. She couldn't believe it. No wonder why Truth always had an issue with her and was always talking his shit; because he wanted her man. Trying to not to throw up inside her mouth. She finally spoke.

"You a sick motherfucker!" Imani screamed. "Why the fuck did you do this?" She yelled at him wanting answers.

"Bitch Adonis already knows why I did it! I love him! He's mine and if he didn't have a little annoying ass bougie bitch annoying the fuck outta him and trying to change him, then he would see that we are meant to be!"

"I told ya'll as soon as I met this nigga that he was sick in the head. NOW do you believe me!?" Nyla interjected. Eyeing her gun, she knew she needed to grab it just in case Truth tried to attack all of them. Adonis was at a loss for words. He was so filled with anger that he just wanted this crazy ass nigga out of his life for good. How could he not see that this nigga was gay? He never even noticed it. I mean Truth was emotional and he fucked a lot of bitches, but he never in a million years would guess that this nigga was on some faggot ass shit. Instantly, he regretted leaving the house not strapped up. If he had his guns on him, this would have never went down. He knew that Truth couldn't have pulled this shit off by himself.

"Who helped you do this Truth?" Adonis asked him

muggin the shit out of him.

"Now you wanna ask the questions?" Truth laughed, "From now on I'll be the one asking the questions." Truth said looking devishly at this them all.

Just as Imani was about to pull her other gun from behind her, two men dressed in all black jumped from out of Truth's closet grabbing Imani and Nyla. Adonis scrambled for the two guns at the bottom.

"Drop em nigga or you will never see this bitch again." Truth threatened.

"Who you think you scaring you trapped in the closet faggot ass nigga!" Adonis screamed.

Just as all hell was about to break loose, gunshots started to ring throughout Truth's condo, and then everything went pitch black.

Chapter 11

Troy was frantically driving around Chicago trying to locate Nyla. It took him a couple hours to sober up and really think about what the fuck he had done. Nyla was the best thing that had ever happened to him, and yet he threw it all away because he was feeling some type of way about her not wanting to have his baby. He was going through a bunch of emotions as soon as he found out that Ivy was Derricks wife. He knew he had to stay in contact with her. Come to find out, she was on the same page as him. She wanted revenge for Louie's death as well. She had cried and told Troy that she knew Louie before she even knew Derrick, and that they had grew up together as children. She didn't understand what would make Derrick kill one of his best friends like it didn't mean shit. When she got word of his death, she immediately made it her business to leave New York and fly out to Chicago. It had been 25 years since she had been to the windy city, and 25 years since she left behind her baby boy. She never meant to hurt Adonis, but she just couldn't be with Derrick anymore. He had become controlling and abusive. He started trying to dictate her every move and whereabouts. She had felt as if she were a child.

A couple of months after Adonis was born, she knew she was gonna have to leave Chicago and start a new life with a new identity. Over the years, she had so many regrets for not taking her only child with her. She hoped that he had become everything that she imagined in her dreams. Troy was in such a rush and so shocked by everything that Ivy was telling him, that he never even got her sons name. Troy didn't care how long it took, he was gonna make it his mission to find Nyla. She had to understand her efforts were appreciated that he fucked up and not her. Before he could try calling her again his cellphone rang it was Ivy calling.

"Ivy what up?" He said wondering what she could want. He told her to keep in contact just in case she found out any information on where Derrick could be hiding.

"I been talking with a few of my old connects out here and I think I can find out where Derrick is. I need your help because I can't do this alone. I don't even want my son to know about me." She said.

Troy wasn't sure how to respond. He didn't know who Derrick was, but he did know one thing, if he came within arms-reach of the man who had murdered his uncle, he wouldn't be able to trust his actions. Before, he had just heard rumors that he was the culprit. Now that Ivy had confirmed it, he knew if he ever came face to face with him he would be a dead man.

"Look I wanna help you ma, but I'm not sure if I can. I wanna see this nigga get the death penalty. If I see him, I might have to take him out myself. I don't want anyone' s blood on my hands." Troy confessed.

Ivy understood where he was coming from, but she knew for a fact that she couldn't take out Derrick alone. When she found out the news in New York, she knew she should have brought back up with her. Because she was so angry, she thought it was a job she could handle by herself. Knowing that she could finally locate him, she didn't give it a second thought. She hadn't seen the nigga in two decades, and she didn't want to risk the chance of Adonis running into her. He had gone all these years without her, and she wanted to keep it that way. Ivy wasn't trying to be selfish, but she had to put him first. Them meeting would only complicate things. She wasn't any better than Derrick to be honest. She had her own share of dealings in the big apple. She didn't want Adonis to feel as if she were a burden if she decided to come into his life.

"I guess I can handle it on my own." Twirling her hair nervously around her fingers she said, "Look Troy I know you don't owe me anything and that we barely know each other, but I want you to know I'm sorry if I caused you any type of pain by telling you the truth. I loved Louie with all of my heart he meant a lot to me. Just in case you do change your mind Imma send you the two addresses where I think he could be." Ivy replied finally letting the situation go.

She didn't wanna force anybody to help her do anything. It was time for her to put on her big girl panties and face Derrick, even if she had to do it alone. Hanging up the phone with Ivy, Troy truly felt as if he was stuck.

He now had the power to take justice into his own hands and kill the motherfucker who had took his uncle from him. He also knew Nyla wouldn't want him to do that, and to let God handle the situation. The only thing that Troy knew was that this shit didn't seem fair to him. His whole life he followed the right path. He wasn't perfect, but he still never went to jail or sold any drugs. If he chose to take matters into his own hands he could not only lose Nyla, but his freedom. *Bleep* a text from Nyla came in it said HELP ME!! In boldfaced caps Troy instantly went into panic mode what the fuck. Dialing her number, she finally answered.

"Nyla where are you? What's wrong baby? Nigga this ain't no damn Nyla. That bitch is dead." CLICK, the phone went dead. Troy's heart dropped. He couldn't recognize the nigga on the other line. Trying to call her phone back, it went straight to voicemail.

"Fuck!" He screamed throwing his phone on the car floor. Just as he was about to lose it, Troy knew that him and Nyla had the same phone. If she could track him then he could track her back. Immediately setting everything up on his phone, he turned on his GPS and sped down the highway.

Chapter 12

Waking up in a cold sweat, Adonis didn't know where he was. The last thing he remembered was hearing gunshots. It sounded like a big ass shoot out with military guns. He remembered reaching out for Imani, but then his world had turned black. Looking around to see where he could be, his vision was blurry. He could see that Imani and Nyla were tied up across from him.

"Imani!!" Adonis frantically called out her name but she wouldn't reply.

"She can't answer. He stuck something in her arm and she been knocked out ever since." Nyla replied with tears strolling down her face.

"Nyla are you able to come to me. I can't really see" Adonis said rubbing his eyes. They burned so badly. Opening them up his vision started to become a bit clearer. Standing up, he saw they were in a dark room that held one glass window. It looked like an interrogation room at a police station. Walking up to the glass trying to see if he could find a way out, he suddenly saw Truth with a group of men sitting behind him.

"Where the fuck are we Truth!!" Adonis screamed in rage. He had enough of Truth's bullshit and games.

"Baby calm down. Now you knew I couldn't let you get away from me that easily." Truth replied. "What did you do to Imani?" Adonis said banging the glass window with his hands.

"Now baby calm down. I just gave her a little sedative to knock her out for a couple of hours. It won't kill her." Truth smirked.

"Damn nigga you are really sprung over this prissy little bitch!" Truth snapped. "She didn't love you, I did! All those years we were taking over Chicago side by side and killed anyone who became a threat to US!! I was there not that bitch Imani." Truth screamed pointing at her through the glass.

Adonis couldn't help to think how sick this nigga really was in the head. He didn't know what type of fantasy he had in his head, but he was about to set this bitch off. One thing Adonis couldn't stand was to be embarrassed. Even though he wasn't a part of The Dynasty anymore, he still had his reputation on the line. He didn't want anyone in the streets thinking he liked a little sugar in his tank. If he could just get on the other side of that glass, he would break Truth's neck. Nyla continued to sob on the floor by Imani. She couldn't believe that Imani had played her like this. All this time she had thought that Adonis was some sort of executive for a law firm downtown, when really he was just the biggest drug king in Chicago. Not only did she feel betrayed, but she also felt bamboozled. Her life was now on the line because of their dangerous lifestyle. Even though he had cheated on her, she still loved Troy and the thought of never seeing him again made her sick to her stomach and caused her to throw up all over the floor.

Truth was disgusted. "The fuck she got going on? Ummmmm what's wrong my dear? You didn't know your friends were little savages did you?" Truth teased. Taking off his shirt, Adonis offered it to Nyla so she could clean herself up. Snatching it away, Nyla just sucked her teeth. She couldn't believe this shit. Here they were being held hostage in a room that straight smelled like urine and shit. Her best friend was dating a drug dealer, and Troy had no idea where she could be at!

"Baby?" Imani whispered starting to wake up. She had no idea where they were. Adonis ran over to her to make sure she was straight. All Truth could do was roll his eyes. He was sure that medication would have knocked her ass clean out. He knew she should have just killed her before they transported. Sucking his teeth, he focused his attention back on Adonis.

"You better stop catering to your little bitch if you wanna get out of here a free man." Truth threatened.

"Nigga I been asking why the fuck would you do this?" Adonis yelled. "Nigga we been boys since I was 15. Why the fuck would you ruin it with this gay shit? You know I will never love you in that way! That shit is sickening! So we can negotiate on whatever it is that you want, but having me is not an option!"

"Just let me suck your dick once then you can decide if you don't want me or not." Truth eyed him trying to seduce him.

"It will be a cold day in hell before I let you touch me!" Adonis warned.

"Oh really we will see about that!" Truth yelled. He was tired of Adonis playing hard to get. He was gonna show Imani how to really give a man head. "Bring him in here." The four men came from the other side of the door grabbing Adonis.

"No please don't hurt him please!" Imani screamed. She took off charging for the door, but the other guy mushed her in the face. Falling down,she frantically tried to catch the door before it closed again only for it to be locked. "No!!!!" She fell against the door in tears.

"Let me go!!" Adonis yelled in rage. "Ya'll don't know who the fuck I am. I will kill all you motherfuckers!" he said trying to break free. It was too many of them.

"Pull that nigga pants off!" Truth ordered. Taking Adonis' arms, they strapped him to the chair and tied his legs up to the chair so he wouldn't be unable to move. Realizing he was stuck, Adonis had to do something that he never thought he would have to do and that was beg.

"Truth please if you ever respected me at all then you won't do me like this." Adonis pleaded. He had never been so scared in his life. Getting on his knees and staring up at Adonis, Truth said "Now baby don't beg. I promise I won't bite."

Placing Adonis' limp dick inside of his mouth, he swirled his tongue around the tip like a popsicle. Adonis let the tears stream down his face, still trying to squirm out of the chair and out of the men's grasp. He started to get mad at his body for the sensations he felt. Imani and Nyla stood against the window in shock. They couldn't believe that Truth was raping Adonis.

Truth turned around to eye Imani, "You will never be able to please him like I can!" Turning back around, Adonis spit dead in Truth's face.

"Nigga you think that's gonna make me stop sucking this big fat dick?" Wiping his face with his shorts, Truth started to take Adonis' whole dick in his mouth, slobbering it down with spit. Truth was a pro at giving head. He had dreamed long before this moment of what it would be like to give Adonis head. The more Truth sucked and licked, the harder it was for Adonis to ignore the pleasure that was coming from his touch. He tried with all his might not to get hard, but he did. Looking at Imani, he mouthed, "I love you and I'm sorry,".

Imani cried her eyes out. She couldn't help it. She felt useless locked on the other side of the door. She knew from the beginning that Truth was trouble and that he would cause nothing but havoc for her and Adonis. Never in a million years did she imagine that he would be that sick in the head. Nyla held Imani's hand. Even though she was pissed at her, she knew that her friend needed her. At the end of the day she loved Imani, and right now they were in a life or death situation. If they were gonna make it out alive, then they had to stick together. All that other shit would have to be put on hold.

"You like me sucking this dick don't you daddy?"

Truth asked. All Adonis could do was close his eyes. Feeling the nut about to rush to the tip of dick he came inside Truth's mouth. Running up to the window like a school girl, Truth spit out the cum for Imani to look at. She was in rage and had enough! Imani frantically looked around the room for something to break the window with. She spotted a chair in the corner. Looking at Nyla, they both were thinking the same thing. Grabbing the chair from both ends. They both lifted It in the air and threw it so hard the whole glass shattered into pieces.

Jumping through the window, Imani grabbed the gun on the counter and started shooting bullets at the two men holding Adonis's arm. On the other side of the room, Nyla had jumped on Truths back and was digging her fingers into his eyeballs.

"Aaaaahhhhh" he screamed in pain!!! Seeing the other two men were down, Imani helped Adonis get out of the chair by untying his legs. Finally able to stand, he took the gun from Imani. Pushing Nyla off of Truth, he grabbed him by his head and slammed him into the wall.

"You crazy ass son of a bitch!!' Adonis roared. Pulling Truth down to the ground, he stuck his knee inside his neck!!! Adonis took the barrel of the gun and hit Truth over and over in the head. Blood escaped his forehead immediately!

"Don't you ever try me on some gay ass shit like that in your life again!" Adonis continued to beat his skull in. Truth was in and out of consciousness.

"Baby please stop!" Imani begged. "He not even worth it!! If you keep beating him, you gonna kill him and go to jail!" Imani saw how bad Truth was beaten, and if Adonis kept going he was gonna kill him.

"Baby come on let' s just leave him and get out of here." Imani pleaded in tears. We can leave Chicago and start our lives over. Adonis looked at Imani and saw all the fear in her eyes. She didn't deserve to keep going through this pain, and if he could give her the world by just leaving all the hell and bullshit behind then he would. Taking his hand, she helped him get off the floor. Hugging him, it felt like time had stopped and it was just the two of them in the room. The past couple of days had been a living nightmare, and now that she was back in his arms again he didn't wanna let go.

"Ummmm hello can we get out of here?" Nyla questioned. She was still scared as hell. They could have their reunion once they got out of this dungeon trap. Looking over at the desk, all of the guns and purses they had were still there. Grabbing everything they could, Imani and Nyla followed Adonis out the building. Finally being able to recognize where they were, Adonis could see that they were being held captive in the abandoned garage behind the warehouse. Neither of them had a car. Everything was still at Truths house! Noticing the keys were still inside of one Truth's Cadillac's that was still in the parking lot, Adonis took it so they could get their cars. If they were gonna leave town, they had to do it fast and in a hurry before someone tracked them down.

Chapter 13

Adonis' mind was going crazy after everything that went down the other night at Derricks garage. Him and Imani were both still in shock from what Truth had put them through. Adonis couldn't erase the image of Truth and his men forcing him to get his dick sucked out of his mind. He was ready to kill Truth. After all of these years of being boys, he would have never suspected that the nigga was gay. Imani had been begging him to leave town and to start a new life giving them both the chance to have a new beginning. The only reason why Adonis was contemplating the idea over in his head was because he knew they would need mad money to just up and leave. He knew he had some money stashed away for a rainy day, but they would need way more loot to make themselves go ghost.

As Imani sat up in the bed, she turned over to wake Adonis up not realizing that he was already awake. "Baby can we just talk about what happened to you?" Imani asked afraid of his response.

"Hell no I told you we never talking about that night. I want you to forget that shit ever happened, do you understand Imani?" He warned her.

"Adonis I know you're a man. I know your pride and your ego feels destroyed. Baby I know that you're hurting, just please don't shut me out." She pleaded with him. If anyone knew his pain, it was her. Imani had been raped while she in foster care by both of her foster parents when she was 17. She knew the effects of what rape could do to a person, especially if they refused to open up and talk about it.

"You can't even begin to imagine how I feel!" he roared punching the wall.

"Yes I do baby. I know because I have been raped

before." Imani stated sadly. She had never told Adonis much about her past. From the moment that she had met him she chose to keep her past life from him because she never wanted him to look at her differently. She always felt it in her heart to make it clear that she wouldn't allow what happened to her to shape her future or her choices. Imani couldn't even call herself a ride or die if she allowed her man to feel guilty over something that was out of his control.

"Look bae Truth turning crazy and being obsessed with you was out of your control. Those thugs holding you down and Truth forcing himself on you wasn't your fault. I know you feel like less of a man but we can't change what happened, we can only move forward. What happened will never change my love for you." Imani said as the tears fell down her face. "When I was 17 and in foster care, both of my foster parents raped me for a year and a half. It wasn't until I told one of my foster parents friends about what went down that he went to the police to report it." Imani said fumbling with the sheets on the silk bed.

In that moment, she felt so vulnerable and more naked in front of him than she had ever felt in the 5 years that they had shared together. He now knew a part of her that she never wanted him to know.

"Imani baby I had no idea, why you never told me about this shit?" He questioned. Adonis never expected for her to tell him some shit like that because they didn't hide things from one another. He figured since it was so deep that maybe she tried to bury what had happened to her from out of her mind.

"I never wanted you to know. You think I wanted you to know that for over a year I let those bastards fuck and suck me however they wanted to? They didn't care about me. They had me brainwashed so badly that I thought it was my fault that they were molesting me every night." She said grabbing Adonis's hands. "The only reason I told you about what happened to me is because I don't want you to feel like you are less of a man because of what those pigs did to you. You are still strong and powerful. Most of all, you're the same Adonis King that saved me all of those years ago. I don't want you to ever forget that." Imani said as she placed his hands over her heart. "You were the first person to value and love me. You didn't abuse me with your words or hurt me physically. You saved me from all the men in my past that I was used to before you. I didn't know what it could be like to have someone treasure me. I will always love you. You are my superman, and nobody can change the way I feel about you Adonis." He couldn't fight the tears that were streaming down his face. He loved this woman, and now that he was at his lowest point he knew truly that she was more than down for him.

"I think we should make a move." Adonis finally spoke. "But I gotta take care of some loose ends before we just take off. "Adonis still hadn't forgotten what Truth had told him before he passed out. If there was a chance that his mother could be in Chicago, he had to at least attempt to find her. He didn't want to let Imani know anything. She was against him finding out where his mother was as well. She could never understand how she could just up and abandon her son like he meant nothing. Adonis decided that if he did end up locating her, then he would let Imani know everything. Right now he didn't want to feel discouraged from searching for her. Derrick had prevented him from doing that for years.

"Okay so here's the plan ma, I'm gonna let you post up at one of my affiliates' house. His name is Shawn. You only gonna be there for a day or two, just until I can get our shit together. Me and him both gonna make sure you good. You won't have to worry about nobody trying to get at you because his crib is gonna be laced with security. Now Shawn is good peoples. He used to help me run all my old territories back in the day. Now that he is retired, he been living it up and he is wealthier than a motherfucker too. I promise you that after I take care of everything, we can jet. We can go to New York.

"New York!" Imani shouted in excitement. She had never been to the big apple. Hearing the name of the city, her mind quickly began to roam with all of the possibilities that could happen for them.

We could change our names, who we are, the whole nine. I just gotta make sure that no one can track us down after we leave this city." Adonis knew he had to make sure that word didn't get back to the police about his involvement in Louie's murder. He didn't want Imani, Nyla, or Troy to figure any shit out.

"What about Truth?" Imani asked. "I know he already out looking for us. If we gonna leave, we gotta get out of Chicago fast. You know that nigga is crazy." She said as she started packing some of her belongings into a suitcase.

"Don't worry about Truth. Fuck him! I think if he knows what's best for him, then he will know to stay out of my path." Adonis said gritting his teeth. "Yo ma I just need you to pack and hurry. Imma drop you off at Shawn spot. I already text him and told him what the deal was." Adonis said as he placed his cellphone back into his pocket.

"Are you sure this gonna all work out babe?" Imani asked looking slightly worried. She wasn't sure she could handle anymore mishaps or fuck ups.

"It has too." Adonis said looking out the condo window. He hoped and prayed to God in that moment that everything went smooth, because if they fucked up it could cost him and Imani everything.

Chapter 14

As Ivy King reached the address that she had set in her GPS, her heart started to pound. She didn't know what to expect. She finally had more than enough evidence and clues to track down her ex-husband. The rage that she felt burned even more inside of her as it did the day she found out Louie was dead. She just couldn't get over the fact that Derrick could be so cruel. Evidently, she never knew the real him. The man that she fell in love with all of those years ago would never kill one of her closest friends. Hell, Louie was the one who introduced the two of them together. He had been one of her closest friends when she was younger. When she first told Louie that she was leaving Derrick, he made a promise that he would never let him know where she was, or even tell Derrick that he knew she planned to walk out on him. For that, she always loved and respected him for keeping her secret. He was the only one who understood why she had to leave her baby behind and the man that she once loved. Derrick had fallen in love with the game more than he did her. She always knew before they got married that Derrick loved getting new pussy. He constantly cheated on her. She naively thought that when they got married, it would satisfy his appetite to step out on her but it only got worse. Derrick demanded that she cut off all her male friends except for Louie. He felt it was okay for him to have his cake and eat it too as long as he took care of home.

Ivy knew that she if she decided to stay with him that nothing would ever change. She didn't want to wake up one day with a million and one regrets, and most of all feeling bitter. Parking on the side of the warehouse, she wanted to be able to creep inside to pop up on Derrick if he happened to be inside. Catching him off guard and unharmed was her best option. Grabbing her gun and pocket knife, she approached the side door and was surprised to see it was already open. Making sure her surroundings were clea,r she noticed right off the back the sound of male voices. Then she heard a voice that sounded all too familiar.

"Listen just find him! I knew that nigga couldn't be trusted!" Derrick yelled at one of his workmen. Truth had gone ghost with up to 40 g's worth of product and cash. As soon as Derrick was able to finally connect the dots, he realized it had been him all along that was stealing from all of his profit. Derrick was furious! He just knew it was something about that faggot Truth that couldn't be trusted. It had been three days since he gave specific orders to transport a shipment to California for him. His connect had received the product from Truth, and had the funds wired to his account instead of Derricks. Pulling up his transaction history in his phone, he saw where the money hadn't been placed in his account. This put The Dynasty in a major hole. Usually when shit went south, Adonis could always come up with a way to get them back twice the money that they had lost but he too was nowhere to be found. For all Derrick knew, both of them motherfuckers could have set him up to take him down.

"I need you niggas to turn this city upside down to find my son and Truth. Them niggas not gonna get away with trying to fucking play me!!" Now that Derrick thought about this shit more, he started to wonder if Adonis saying he was going to leave The Dynasty could have been just a major distraction to throw him off from what him and Truth were really doing. Throwing the Hennessey bottle against the wall, Derrick sucked his teeth. How could he have been so stupid. His son was just as much of a snake as his mother. Two selfish people who only gave a fuck about themselves. As she heard the mention of her son being in danger, Ivy knew she had to make her presence known. It was no way in hell she was going to let Derrick King hurt her son, not on her watch.

"Stop right there!" Ivy pointed her gun at Derrick and his work men. He couldn't believe it. Was it really Ivy? His mind immediately flashed to the day that they first met, the first time they made love, the moment she told him that she was indeed carrying his seed, and the moment that they took their wedding vows as man and wife. Then he remembered that this was the same woman who had left him and Adonis and never once looked back.

All the years that had went by, she never tried to reach out to get in contact with him or their son. She was the reason why his heart had grown so cold. Ivy took vows to love and honor him for better and for worse, and she couldn't even uphold her end of the promise she made on that day. He knew he had been unfaithful, but what young nigga wouldn't be. No matter how many bitches he had been with, he always made sure to take care of home. At the end of the day, that was then and this was now. It was too late to apologize. Neither of the old lovers spoke at first. Ivy was shocked to see him in a wheelchair. At least she knew she didn't have to worry about him trying to attack her. She now held all the power because she had no problem knocking off the niggas who were after her son.

"I want everyone out!" Derrick demanded never taking his eyes off of Ivy.

"These thugs, your little hit men ain't going nowhere if it's to hurt my son!!" She warned him still aiming her gun at them.

"Oh now he's your son?" Derrick asked becoming more pissed off by the second. "I raised your son with my blood, sweat and tears. Don't you try to come busting up in my place of business after 20 years talking about protecting your damn son. Bitch you got some nerve!"

Derrick yelled ready to attack her. He hated his wheelchair was holding him back from choking the shit out of her. He never felt so disrespected in his life. Ivy had no idea how much pain she took him through. The only thing that she cared about was herself. Even after all these years she still was the same selfish ass bitch.

"Like I said, you call off your manhunt or I'll shoot them all dead. Please don't fuck with me!" She demanded. Realizing he had to play her game, at least for the time being, he decided to give in for now.

"Ya'll go find Truth. I'll handle Adonis myself. If you touch him, you will have to answer to me." Derrick warned the two men.

"Ya'll can go." Ivy said putting down the gun releasing them. They nearly flew out the warehouse. They knew that bitch didn't have no problem busting a cap in their ass.

"So Ivy what are you really doing here?" Derrick questioned looking her over. He was still pissed off with her, but damn she was still fine as hell. Her ass stayed fat and only got better with age.

"Don't you dare try to question me! Especially after you killed Louie! I know everything!" Ivy shouted at Derrick.

"Well you might have heard wrong, I didn't kill Louie. I'm still trying to figure out who knocked him off my damn self." Derrick said taking puff out of his cigar. She knew for a fact that he was lying, but he wasn't gonna admit to what he did. Ivy was pissed and he was handicapped. If he told her the truth, she could very well kill him dead on the spot. She had perfect opportunity and motive.

"Don't try to play me like I'm stupid!!" Ivy said pulling the trigger back on the gun. She was fully prepared to show this nigga what time it was. "You knew how much

Louie meant to me. He was like my brother and you took him away!" Ivy stressed to him. All of the emotions she kept guarded up came rushing out at that very moment. "It was already fucked up that I had to leave my whole life, my child, my family, just to get away from your controlling ass. Louie was the only piece to Chicago that I still had to hold onto." Ivy said trying to hold back her tears. She didn't want to come off as weak in front of Derrick.

"You mean to tell me that all this time you still had been keeping in contact with Louie ass and he didn't even tell me?" Derrick asked completely thrown for a loop.

"Don't be mad with him. Louie was a loyal man. He never once turned his back on me!!" Ivy wanted to kill Derrick so bad for taking her friend away from her, but she couldn't bring herself to pull the trigger. She was angry, but yet part of her just wanted to understand why Derrick operated the way he did. Not only had he turned on his day one, but now his son was his next target. After everything was all said and done, she left Chicago. She knew that if she would have taken Adonis with her, it wouldn't take Derrick much longer to come back after Adonis with full force again. Before they could finish conversing back and forth, Truth stumbled into the backdoor of the warehouse from the abandoned garage. He appeared to be bloody and his left eyes was swollen shut.

"Who is this?" Ivy asked pointing the gun at Truth.

"Please don't shoot!!' Truth moaned. He was in severe pain. His men were dead inside the garage where he had taken Nyla, Imani, and Adonis hostage just the day before. Truth had been unconscious for at least 24 hours. He had just mustered up just enough energy to walk to the warehouse. Still feeling woozy, he immediately collapsed on the chair nearby.

"Who did this to you?" Derrick asked pretending to be concerned.

"Adonis. He attacked me and stole all of your money". Truth replied throwing Adonis under the bus. Hell, he deserved it for choosing that bitch over him! Although he still loved him deeply, it was fucked up how he beat his ass.

"Stop lying on my son you pig." Ivy interrupted him. She had no idea who this young boy was, but it was no way she was gonna allow his rat ass try to snitch on her baby boy.

"We can settle this right now. I will call Adonis and tell him to meet me now!" Derrick said finally fed up. He wanted his money and was gonna get it one way or another.

"No!" Ivy panicked. She wasn't done getting her answers she needed from Derrick, and she really wasn't ready to be face to face with her son.

"Look bitch I don't care what type of shit you on, If I need to speak to my son I will. I don't need to ask for permission when I'm a grown ass man." Derrick told her looking at her as if she had lost her damn mind. As the two of them were going back and forth, a voice interrupted and stopped them all.

"I ain't running now motherfucker. If you want me, come get me. Ain't no way in hell you gonna take me down for the shit you and this faggot set me up to do!" Adonis said pointing at Truth.

"Son!" Ivy could barely get the words out as she saw her son face to face for the first time in over two decades.

"Momma!?" Adonis questioned not believing it was really her. As soon as he started to embrace her, shots rang out throughout the entire warehouse and all hell had broken loose.

Chapter 15

Nyla was truly thankful for still being alive. After what went down with Imani, Adonis, and Truth she was angry at first. She quickly got over it though because she knew she couldn't stay mad at Imani for too long. She had been her friend through all the up's and downs, and even though she did lie it didn't change the fact that she was still her best friend. We all made mistakes. Nyla was willing to forgive her. Troy had been trying to reach her ever since she came back from her ordeal. Ever since that terrible night, she had been feeling sick to her stomach and finally worked up the nerve to take an at home pregnancy test. Placing the opened test on the bathroom counter she already had her urine sitting in the cup. She couldn't build up the courage to dip the stick inside. For so long she was resistant and firm in her decision on not having a baby, but now she was unsure of what to feel, especially after Troy had cheated on her. What if she really was pregnant? Didn't she owe it to herself and her baby to try to work things out with Troy.?

"Okay Nyla breathe." She said to herself trying to calm her nerves as she placed the stick inside the urine. Placing the dipped stick on to the paper towel, she silently said a prayer to herself. She hoped to God that she wasn't pregnant. It just wasn't the right time at all. As soon as she opened her eyes to look at the test, she saw a big fat positive pop up.

Well there it was plain as day. Nyla couldn't help but to burst into tears. She had no idea what she was gonna do. She knew without a doubt that she just had to consider abortion or adoption and not tell Troy shit. Sitting on the toilet, she heard her doorbell rang. Peeping through the hole, it was just her type of luck to see Troy's trifling ass on her doorstep. "Go away Troy!!" Nyla yelled through the door.

She still wasn't ready to have a sit down conversation with him. In the two years that they had been together, she never once cheated on him. Her heart was really hurting and she didn't wanna say anything to him that she may regret later.

"Baby you text me talking about help you the other night." Troy replied worried. After he tried to locate her the other night, he was unable to find her. Since her phone was dead the I-Phone wouldn't take him to her destination. For two days he had been sick not knowing whether was in trouble or okay. 'Can you just please let me in so we can talk about this on the inside? Nyla I need to know where we stand. I can't go through this another day. I know a nigga fucked up, but how can I even make shit right if you keep me at a distance ma?" He pleaded on the other side of her door. He felt like he was begging for his life, hell Nyla was his life. She didn't deserve the bullshit that he was taking her through. Nyla didn't know what to do. Even though she was still highly pissed, she decided to at least hear him out for what it was worth. Opening the door to let him inside her apartment, he attempted to hug her but she pushed him away.

"Look we can talk and that's it." Nyla said her voice lacking compassion. She wanted Troy to feel guilty as hell for what he had done. For two years he had her and the world fooled as if he was the perfect guy, when he just like all these other niggas thinking with their dick instead of their head.

"I know you're upset bae and I can explain everything if you just let me." Troy said preparing his explanation in his head. Sitting on her sofa, he sighed before continuing to speak.

"Oh so you know her name now." Nyla said shaking her head.

"Can you just let me finish?" He said becoming irritated.

"That night at the bar when I met Ivy, I was all fucked up. I mean here I was dealing with the loss of my uncle who meant the world to me. You out of all people should know how much I loved him. He was there for me more than my own father was. So to have him just be killed by some asshole and his body be dumped in the car like he was some type of stray dog really fucked with my head, and it still does. I went out with only the intentions to drink my problems away. I needed time to myself, and all you wanted to do was nag me about going out and drinking when I just needed that alone time."

"So now you trying to throw this shit on me?" Nyla stated looking at him as if she was disgusted.

"No I'm not trying to throw it on you, but come on Nyla. You kept bugging thinking I was going to do something crazy, and yeah maybe I was and still do. Whoever killed my uncle is gonna have hell to pay. I'm not letting that shit go. I wanted to tell you how I was feeling but I knew you wouldn't see shit my way. You would have just said let the police handle it. Which I refuse to do." He said looking her dead in the eyes.

"You are really gonna throw your whole life away just because you feel like you gotta take matters into your own hands? My god why Troy. I mean what is that really gonna solve? You willing to go to jail just to prove a point. You ain't as smart as I thought you were. The man that I met would never kill someone else or talk the way you talking. It's stupid and I don't care what you felt. It's no excuse for you to fuck somebody else. All I was doing was trying to be a good woman and check on you and be there for you and what do you do? Go get drunk and fuck some random bitch!" She said getting heated all over again. "I want to forgive you but I don't think I can. It's too much too soon. I really just am not ready to forgive and forget." She said feeling final in her decision.

Nothing that Troy said made any sense. His reason for cheating on her was stupid and there was no telling the next time something major went down that he wouldn't cheat on her again. "You can get the rest of your things later and let yourself out." She said getting off of her sofa and heading back up the stairs.

"So that's just it? We over like that?" Troy asked feeling defeated. He didn't want it to end this way. Without Nyla he had no life. He wanted her to one day be his wife and the mother of his kids. The thought of them being over for good would definitely send him over the edge.

"Baby please don't give up on us we can fix this." In that moment, Nyla knew she could have mentioned the baby. Maybe then he wouldn't be so driven to get revenge on his Uncle's killer. She quickly dismissed the idea. She couldn't just agree to have a baby to make him happy or forgive him like nothing happened. She needed time apart to figure everything out.

'I need time away from you Troy. Time to figure out if this relationship is even worth saving. Please just go." She said walking up the stairs leaving him standing alone. Looking around her living room, Troy knew he had to be a man and give her the space she needed. He could only blame himself for where they stood with one another. He could continue to beg for her to take him back, but his pride wouldn't let him. He just had to let the water run dry. Making sure to lock her door before leaving out, he grabbed a couple of his belongings and left. Nyla secretly stood outside her bedroom window and watched him pull out her driveway. She hated that she had to let him go, but the worth she had for herself just wouldn't give her the ability to give him a second chance. Closing her blinds, she realized all she had left was a broken heart and piece of Troy inside of her womb.

Chapter 16

Imani had been trying to get in contact with Adonis since she got settled at Shawn's penthouse. Even though she didn't feel completely safe there, she knew she had to let Adonis get things in order so they could leave town. She had the whole pad to herself. Even though Shawn was retired, he did a lot of running in and out. Imani was truly exhausted. She didn't get a lot of rest and was suffering mad anxiety since being held hostage Truth. Trying to think of happy thoughts she instantly dreamed of what her life would be like in New York with Adonis. Since she was a young girl she always wanted to go there and at least visit and just the thought of living there made me excited with all the new possibilities she would be experiencing. Hearing footsteps approaching the door, Imani immediately became scared. Shawn walked into the room wondering why she looked so freaked out.

"Aye you good?" He asked. "You ain't gotta be worried about nothing while I'm here. I promised Adonis that I would look out for you while he takes care of his business. I gave him my word and I meant that." Shawn looked her over. Damn Imani was beautiful. Not wanting to overstep his boundaries, he quickly shook the thought out of his head. Imani started to relax. It was something in Shawn's voice that made her feel secure and safe. She knew that she would be good at least until Adonis got done with whatever he needed to do.

"I'm straight I guess. Look I have been trying to get in contact with Adonis, but he hasn't answered. Has he been in contact with you at all?" Imani asked.

"Yeah he text me about an hour ago and told me he would hit you up around 5." Shawn told her.

"Okay cool," she said feeling much better. It was only 3pm, so she knew everything has to be going as planned. Deciding to chill and enjoy her new living quarters, she decided to strike up a conversation with Shawn. She wished she could call Nyla, but decided to lay low and give her the space that she needed.

"So why you in this big ass pad alone?" Imani asked Shawn as she opened herself a cold sprite from the mini fridge inside the room. She was curious and wondered why would a man like a Shawn live in this big ass house alone. He had no girlfriend or wife, and it wasn't like he was ugly. Imani just always figured that there was somebody for everybody.

"I try to stay low ley as possible ma." Shawn explained not trying to go into heavy detail. He didn't like for people to pry in his business. He could tell that Imani would try to talk his head off. Opening up a 6 pack of Corona's, he decided to play her game. Shit if he had to babysit her while Adonis was away, he might as well have a little fun with her.

"How long and my man been rocking?" He asked chugging the ice cold beer down.

"We been together 5 years." Imani said smiling to herself.

"That's what's good. You love him?" Shawn asked being nosey. Imani was sexy as hell. He wondered if she was one of them wifey types that stayed true to her man, or was she the type that knew how to have a good time and go back to her dude like nothing happened. He hadn't had some good pussy in a while. He figured he might as well try to get a little extra compensation for a job well done.

"Yes I do love my man." Imani smirked trying to blow him off. All of a sudden, she started to not feel as comfortable as she did before. Maybe trying to talk to Shawn wasn't a good idea.

"You hungry?" Shawn asked. "I'm 'bout to order up some Chinese food. I know you gotta be starving by now."

"I'm good for now." Imani really was starving but she didn't like the vibe that Shawn was giving her. It made her feel like he was trying to check her out or be on some foul shit.

"Ok suit yourself. I'll be back." He said closing the door to his guest room.

Imani paced back and forth in the room unsure of what to do. Usually when she felt an intuition about something, she couldn't ignore it. Now seemed like one of those times. She didn't know what type of game Shawn was trying to play, but she wasn't some thot ass trick. She just wanted to make conversation because she was bored. Sitting on the edge of the bed, her phone started to go off. It was Adonis.

"Yo ma everything good?" Adonis asked breathing heavily.

"Yeah I'm good. What's wrong babe you sound out of breath?"

Look we may have to leave out in about 24 hours. Some crazy shit just went down at my pops warehouse, and I think my mother set the whole thing off.

"Wait bae did you say you mother? What you mean? Is she in Chicago." Imani couldn't process what she was hearing. Why would Adonis' mom come back to town after all of these years. After everything she put him through, she might as well have just stayed gone. One thing she didn't like was a sorry ass parent. She knew that pain all too well dealing with the loss of her father abandoning her at a young age. For years, she watched as Adonis yearned for the truth about his mother. She didn't want to see him set himself up for failure only to be let down in the end.

"You need to come to Shawn's so we can talk. Are

you sure you not hurt?" She asked.   "Yeah look I gotta go with my gut Imani. That riot was staged, and I know for a fact that my mom is here in Chicago. I owe it to myself to at least hear what she gotta say. She went ghost as soon as the shots rang out, and I gotta locate her before she just up and leave town again."

"Adonis how do you know she even wants to be found? Imani pressured him. "You gotta think smart don't be on some sucker shit! This woman been MIA your whole life, and all of sudden she back in Chicago. For what purpose? I don't think she has your best interest at heart, and we don't need any distractions fucking up our plans to go to New York. Adonis are you listening to me?" She asked becoming irritated. His mind was gone. He finally had the chance to be face to face with his mom's, but then she went ghost. He wondered if it was her doing or someone else's'. Either way, he couldn't just shake it off. Adonis didn't know if he would ever have the opportunity to confront his mother again.

He had always only known what his father had placed in his ear from the time that he was a child. Now he wanted to know his mother's side of the story. What would make her just up and leave her child, and why couldn't he have just taken him with her? The story just didn't make sense. Believe it or not, somewhere deep inside, he was trying to give her the benefit of the doubt.

"Imani if you love me can you just please support me on this? I promise if I can't find her, I will let this go." He said promising to at least try to stay true to his word.

"Ugh ok Adonis. 24 hours! I'm not playing. I'm here waiting on you. I love you and please be careful. Remember we going to NYC."

"I know baby. Just lay low at Shawn's and remember what I said about your phone. No calling Nyla or anyone else except me until I come scoop you up. I don't need anyone to know where you at." He told her making sure that she understood.

"I got you." She decided not to say anything about Shawn. She knew how to handle shit if something were to pop off. Hanging up, she laid on the bed and envisioned her life with Adonis and moving to New York and becoming his wife. No one was going to tear them apart, not even the people they knew in the crazy streets of Chicago.

Chapter 17

Mya sat in her hotel room chuckling to herself. Her plan had gone without a hitch, thanks to her brother Smitty. After paying him a chunk of her earnings from kidnapping Adonis the other night, she was fully able to set off her operation. She never had any intentions of leaving Chicago to begin with. Yes, Truth had broken her off with a nice piece of change, but in reality she knew that the money would soon run out. The idea to rob Derrick was clever. She would have never thought of it had her brother not convinced her it was the smart thing to do. The plan was to bust in Derrick's warehouse and set it off with a whole bunch of smoke bombs. Thanks to Mya knowing exactly where Adonis and Derricks had kept their stash, Smitty and his partners were able to locate it fast. Mya knew that Derrick literally kept his whole life in that safe. He had maps of all his old and new territories inside the safe and codes to all of his off shore accounts. Plus, a full list of all of his connects with numbers and addresses. She couldn't wait to be able to take over The Dynasty with Smitty as her right hand man.

Derrick has to be stupid to not put him on from the jump. Smitty had a quality that Truth lacked. He killed without hesitation and never left any tracks to get caught up in any bullshit. He would have been a way better co-conspirator then Truth had been to Adonis.

"Did you take care of it?" She answered her brothers call on the first ring.

"Yeah we took care of that sis." He replied legit amazed that everything went down smoothly. He couldn't lie, he thought his sister was bluffing on getting shit done but she actually kept up her end of the bargain.

"Did you make sure to grab everything and not

hurt anybody?' She asked worried that her brother might have done something crazy. All she wanted was to hit Derrick where it hurt the most and that was by hurting his pockets. Without money and no power, he couldn't run The Dynasty to its full capacity. Especially without Adonis there to cover up his fucks up. Just like Truth had let the tracks be uncovered back to them for Louie's murder. Smitty would have never done any dumb shit like that. He was always on point with whatever he did. If he had a body on his hands, best believe it would never turn back up. He aimed to kill and dismiss with a vengeance.

"We got all the goods! All we did was rough your man up a little bit he'll live." Smitty replied un-phased. He knew that she was only trying to make sure that Derrick was still breathing. He didn't get why Mya was still trying to look out for this nigga. She was really being stupid and he hated that shit. Derrick had already said that he didn't want anything to do with her, so would she still continue to care about him was beneath him. One thing he didn't want for his sister to be a sucker or a needy ass chick. That's why when Derrick didn't want him to be on The Dynasty he wasn't tripping about it. Shit he could start his own shit off without his help or money. Yet and still, his sister thought she would have the upper hand since she was giving him the pussy.

"Smitty chill bro I told you to move in and move out. Why you always gottta be hard headed?" Mya said worried that he might have seriously hurt Derrick.

"Naw you need to chill. I just did you a major favor and the only thing you can do is bitch and complain and worry if this nigga hurt or not. You just robbed the nigga blind so how you gonna act like you give a fuck about his well-being." Smitty said sucking his teeth. She had some nerve to be unappreciative after what they just did. Smitty was taking a huge risk. He was just getting started in the game and he knew he would have to earn his street cred and respect. Crossing The Dynasty was a huge risk that he was taking as a newcomer to the game. He had to make sure that the shit was kept under wraps about him or any of his people being involved in the robbery. He refused to be sloppy with his moves.

"Look can you just calm down? I appreciate you bro no doubt. I just don't want to see you go down for a murder charge or going back to jail period. I'm trying to run up this money." Mya said getting excited about the possibility of being the new head bitch in charge. She was gonna make sure that before the week was over with that Derrick had turned on all of his associates and flipped the script on them. Making way for Smitty and his squad to be the new town Drug leaders. With her and Smitty running the city, they would be unstoppable. Brushing her fingers through her hair, Mya looked in the mirror as she talked to her brother.

"What time you gonna able to meet me? She asked. Mya was eager to meet him as soon as possible to make sure he hadn't forgotten anything behind inside of Derricks safe.

"I can be over that way in about an hour." He asked growing impatient.

"Damn an hour? Why so long?" She asked knowing she was being extra, but she didn't give a damn.

"Look I gotta make a stop before I come through. Why you so jumpy sis? Damn if you gonna be rocking with me on some business type shit you gotta have faith. I know I'm new to this, but trust me. You gotta have faith that I got this shit on lock!" He said stressing his point so she could get it.

"I know I'm sorry if it feels like I'm tripping on you. I just wanna make sure that we can be successful in our future plans. I'll see you in about an hour."

Hanging up the phone, Smitty smiled to himself. He hated that he was gonna have to take matters into his own hands. He had all the info he needed from Derrick and 60'gs worth of cash, which was more than enough to start his own empire. It was only room for one person to be at the top. He didn't have time to share the wealth. He was greedy and wanted it all. The sooner he could get his sister out of the picture, the better. Mya was too hung up and in love with Derrick to completely turn on him. She nearly flipped her fucking wig when she found out that Smitty had laid his paws on him to rob the safe. Suppose one day she just tried to run back to Derricks arms if he was willing to fuck with her again. Smitty didn't have room for any confusion or half ass loyalty.

There was no love in this business. Making sure he had all the shit he would need, he prepared his next move to be his next move yet.

"Sorry sis but I gotta do what's for the best." He said blowing the smoke from the cigarette out of his mouth. Smitty Williams will be the new head drug lord of Chicago.

Chapter 18

Imani stood in Shawn's kitchen tearing up the orange chicken with shrimp fried rice he had ordered for her. Even though she told him that she wasn't hungry, he still had gone out and got her something to eat. She was trying to hurry up and eat and go back to the guest room before he popped up back to his house. Deciding to keep her distance from him for the rest of her stay, she hoped she could avoid any misunderstandings.

"Damn that food hit the spot." She said to herself as she stood in the refrigerator looking for a cold drink to wash her meal down with. As soon as she closed the door, Shawn had popped up from behind it.

"Oooh shit!" She screamed as she dropped the glass of wine on the floor. Glass had shattered everywhere.

"Yo my fault I didn't mean to scare you I thought you had heard me come in." He said apologizing.

"Hell no." She said freaked out.

"Well I'll just get out of your way then." Imani said trying to get back to her room.

"It ain't no need for all that." Shawn said staring at her intensely. Now was the best time to make his move on her. Adonis had already hit him up and told Shawn he was gonna be picking up Imani in two or three days which meant he had to make his quick. "I could be wrong but I think you feeling me." Shawn countered her as Imani tried to walk backwards to get away from him. The closer he got, the more uncomfortable she became.

"Look Shawn, I don't know what type of vibe you getting. I appreciate you for helping my man out by letting me crash here while he takes care of business, but that's all this is. I'm not that kind of female." She said watching his every move.

"Imani ain't nothing to be scared of. What Adonis don't know won't hurt him. Knowing she was in trouble, Imani quickly took off running upstairs. She knew Shawn wasn't far behind.

"Please just leave me alone." She pleaded trying to close the door on him.

"Bitch stop fighting me. You knew you couldn't stay here for free." He roared through the door. Shawn hadn't had any pussy in a minute. His dick throbbed at the thought of fucking Imani without her man knowing. As many times as he looked out for him in the past, he could at least be generous and share his bitch too.

Pushing the door down with all of his force, he grabbed Imani by the hair and shoved her down on the bed.

"No!" she screamed. Imani was terrified. It was as if history was repeating itself.

"Open your legs. Don't make me knock your ass out." Shawn warned.

"Hell no motherfucker! Get off of me." She screamed back.

"Okay so you wanna play hard to get." Shawn said. Becoming pissed, he smacked her hard on the face. Ripping her panties off, he quickly flipped her her over on all fours and stuck his fingers inside her asshole.

"Owwww!!!" She yelled out. "Please don't! I have never had anal sex before please don't do this to me Shawn!!!" She sobbed.

"Shut the fuck up bitch you gonna give me this ass!" He said forcefully shoving her face inside the silk pillows. Without any lube, Shawn spit on his fingers and put the saliva on his rock hard dick as he rammed his big dick inside of her virgin ass hole.

"NOOOOOOO OMG!!! Please someone help me!" She cried. She could feel the blood pour from her swollen ass.

Imani tried her best to fight him off but to no avail. "Please!" She whimpered as she felt herself start to go in and out of it. She was in such severe pain. Shawn was in bliss. He felt like he was so high. Imani truly had some good shit. Fucking her ass as rough as he could, he ignored her cries. If she had just been willing to give it to him willingly he wouldn't have had to take it. Imani prayed to herself that he would hurry up and finish. She was in a true nightmare. She had a feeling that staying with Shawn would be a bad idea, and here she was paying the ultimate price.

"Turn over!" He demanded grabbing the cloth beside the nightstand to wipe the blood that stained his dick. He slowly re-entered himself into her dry walls. She felt no attraction to Shawn at all.

Pressing all of his body weight on her, Imani felt as if she were gonna throw up at any second. Shawn smelled of old spice and musty ass all rolled into one.

"Ooooohh shit girl you got some good..." BANG, BANG, BANG, BANG, BANG. Adonis walked into the room firing the shots into Shawn's back. He kept trying to shoot more but his gun had run out of bullets. Rushing over to Imani, he pulled Shawn's dead body off of his queen.

"Oh my God ma I'm so sorry." He said picking her up into his arms.

"Baby..." she said in tears. "He raped me! Oh god noooooo!" She cried. Imani was frantic and couldn't calm down. She had hoped that their troubles would be over and that they could be worry free. He saw that her face was swollen and that blood was dripping from her insides. "Ma come on I gotta get you to a hospital!!" He said attempting to take her downstairs.

"No!" she said beginning to panic. "If we go to the hospital, they are gonna ask questions and it will lead the police over here. Then you will go to jail for murdering

Shawn."

"Imani baby you're in pain. My God you've just been raped! What type of nigga would I be if I just let this slide? I gotta make sure you good. You need to see a doctor now!" He said glaring at Shawn's cold corpse on the hardwood floor, "I can't believe this fuck nigga pulled this bullshit! Imani baby I'll never be able to forgive myself for letting this happen to you." he cried holding his head in his hands. "Fuck I can't deal he hurt my wife!? he roared kicking Shawn's body over and over. Trying to appear strong in front of him, Imani quickly tried to stand up on her own.

"Adonis calm down please! I just need a minute and a shower. I gotta clean up and wash this shit off of me. I'll be good. I just need a moment to regroup." Imani anticipated wiping her face off. I'm not gonna let you get caught up in any trouble it's no way you going to jail for killing this pathetic bastard."

Pulling her into his arms he begged Imani to not be mad at him. He felt so responsible for her being attacked. He should have known not to let her stay with Shawn. Had he not been so selfish and eager to locate his mother and run the streets, he could have saved her from this pain.

"I just wanna shower." Imani said staring at him. Her eyes held no sparkle to them She looked like she lost all of the hope inside of her beautiful brown eyes. "I wanna go home after I get dressed." She said closing the bathroom door. Adonis knew she was upset. He felt so guilty for leaving her with Shawn. He had to think smart. As soon as he dropped Imani off, he would have to come back to Shawn's place, clean up, and dispose the body. Adonis still wanted to search for his mother, but right now he was going to have to make Imani his prime focus. He promised to get them out of Chicago, and he was gonna keep his word. Not making her his first priority is what led them to this bullshit in the first place. Hearing her turn the shower off, he quickly gave her an outfit to throw on and her shoes. The faster he could drop her off at the crib, the sooner he could come back to clean up the place. Making sure not to leave any of her belongings behind, she followed Adonis to his charger so they could go home. The whole ride home they barely spoked. Imani just knew that her time in Chicago was up. If Adonis didn't make something shake soon, she was gonna have to leave him. His choices we putting her in the most dangerous of situations. Never in a million years did she think she would ever have to contemplate making that choice. The past few weeks had shown her just how fast being a King-Pins girlfriend would ruin her life. It just had to be away for them to both be saved from the fuckery and despair.

Chapter 19

Ivy sat on the train headed back to New York feeling empty. She had come to Chicago with one goal in mind, only for all of her plans to be shot to hell. She couldn't get the image of Adonis out of her head. It was remarkable how much he looked like her. It was as if they could have been twins. The only thing he gained from Derrick was his tall height. When the shots and smoke bomb went off in the warehouse, she had run to her car and took off. She didn't know who or what was coming for Derrick, but she didn't want any parts of it. She also knew that if she stayed in town, it wouldn't be long before Adonis or Derrick came trying to track her down if they hadn't started already. Ivy was not ready to take the responsibility for leaving her son behind, and she felt like a coward for it. Maybe in another life time she would be able to rebuild the broken relationship between her and Adonis. For now, she had to think of a Plan B to get back at Derrick for murdering Louie in cold blood. Closing her eyes and trying to gather her thought's while listening to the train tracks click, she got a beep in on her cellphone. Reading the message, it said, "I'm on to you," from a number she didn't recognize or have saved in her phone.

"Who is this?" She replied.

"Derrick bitch you not getting away for setting me up. I will kill you!"

Staring at her phone in fear, she wondered how Derrick couldn't even get a hold of her cellphone number. If he had that, could it possibly be tracked to let him know of her location.

"Don't text me again motherfucker. I don't do threats, only promises!" She text him back trying to scare him off. Beep her phone went off again

"Word to the wise, it's never a threat with me only a promise!" He said.

Ivy quickly turned her phone off and started checking her surroundings. Everything seemed straight. She had to make a clean break as soon as she got back to New York. Whatever Derrick was up to, he wouldn't give up until he located her. She had to be 10 steps ahead of him. She had to remain calm and cool because at the end of the day, she had more leverage than Derrick since he was handicapped.

Trying to take her mind to a happy place, she instantly thought of Troy. Even though they had just shared one night with each other, she couldn't stop thinking about him. She knew he had a girl at home, but she felt a connection with him. That was weird because she didn't know him for long. Maybe it was the fact that he was related to Louie which made her feel so close to him. She hoped that day that she text Troy the information to Derricks whereabouts, that he would follow her lead and join her or at least go on his own to handle Derrick. Maybe he would use all of information she gave him to his advantage now that she was gone.

"Ma'am, would you care for another beverage?" The attendant asked.

"Yes I would like a margarita on the rocks." she said. Desperately, she wished she could have a glass of Jack Daniels to take her off the edge and cure her lonely thoughts. As the train made a stop, new travelers were coming aboard as well. As the waitress came back with her drink, she started to sip on her margarita waiting for them to pull off again. A couple of sips in, she saw a handsome dark skinned man board the train. The closer he came towards the back the more and more he looked and sounded like Troy. "Omg its him!" She said under her breath excited! What could he be doing here she wondered?

"Troy!" She yelled out getting his attention.

"Ivy?" He questioned surprised that they were on the same train. "What are you doing here?" He asked.

"I'm headed back to New York! I told you that's where I live now." She said. "Where are you headed?" She wondered. "I see you are alone." she added.

"Yeah well umm, Nyla found out about what happened between us and she told me she needs her space. So I packed up my things and left." He said looking out the train window still debating if he was making the right decision.

"You sound like you not too sure about going?" Ivy replied.

"To be honest, I'm not. But I'm not about to beg her to take me back. I know I fucked up, but she could have at least tried to give me the benefit of the doubt." he said trying to defend his actions.

"Well I mean you did cheat." Ivy reminded him.

"Yes I know what happened between us was wrong, but you played a part in it too." Troy added.

"Okay but I was not in a relationship with Ms. Nyla, you were. You chose to fuck up your relationship not me! I didn't put a gun to your head so that you will feel forced to fuck me!" She hissed under her breath. She didn't want to draw any attention towards them.

"All I'm saying is that I was going through a tough time. It's hard for me to still deal with the fact that my Uncle is gone. So while I'm gone, I'm going to give myself time to heal. Leaving Chicago is the best thing for me to do. Especially before I do something that's out of my nature."

"So you didn't use the addresses that I gave you." Ivy said shaking her head.

"I thought about it. Hell I'm still thinking about it, but somebody reminded me about not taking justice into my own hands. I don't want to lose my life or end up in prison trying to look for revenge."

"So that's just it. We are supposed to just let Derrick get away with what he did to Louie? He took him from our lives forever!" Ivy was pissed. It was no way in hell she was gonna roll over and let Derrick win or walk away free with blood on his hands. It wasn't fair. Derrick had enough power to make it look like someone else took Louie out, so that way he wouldn't have to take the fall. He was pussy and to know him was to hate him.

"I can't even believe you. If you loved Louie, you wouldn't want to see his killer walk away without dying for his actions." Ivy said in tears. "The hood is full of niggas everyday dying without never getting justice for their deaths Troy. I refuse to let Louie's death go in vain." She stared deeply into his eyes.

Troy didn't know what to say. He had to make peace with Louie being gone in his own way. The reason he was going to New York was to clear his mind from all the hate and anger he felt. If him and Nyla were ever going to pick up from where they left off, he had to become the man she fell in love with again.

"I don't want to keep talking about this Ivy. If you will excuse me, I gotta find my seat." He said grabbing his bag and leaving her feeling dumbfounded. Not knowing where they stood with one another, Ivy wished that she had the ability to just forgive and forget, but it wasn't in her nature she was built to seek and destroy all those who crossed her. She sighed to herself looking out the window as the train continued its journey.

Chapter 20

Truth couldn't believe he was in this position. Here he laid at The University of Chicago Medicine Hospital, in physical and emotional pain. Not only from the bruises that covered his body, but from the scars that were left on his heart. He never expected for Adonis to react to the fact that he loved him the way he did. He honestly felt like deep down inside, that the same way that he had loved him for all of these years, was maybe how Adonis had felt. Had he missed the signs or just blind from his own ignorance? He never meant to force himself on Adonis, but he had to show him that with him was where he needed to be. He could try deny his affection all that he wanted, but he felt the way his dick got harder and harder in his mouth as he stroked it with his tongue. There was no denying the cum that burst in his mouth as Adonis ejaculated. It still had to be away for him to convince Adonis that they belonged together, but he couldn't do a damn thing until he healed first. Pressing the button to call the nurse into his room, he desperately needed some more pain meds to handle the pain he was in. Adonis had given him a royal ass whooping, but he just shrugged it off as bae was in his feelings. He knew he had taken things overboard by kidnapping him and his little bitch and her crybaby ass friend, but they were the ones who came looking for Adonis. It wasn't as if he came fucking with them.

"Yes sir can I help you?" The nurse asked coming into his room.

"Yes I need some more damn meds. My back is killing me." He said moaning in pain. Looking into the drawer next to him, he got his cellphone and worked up the courage to call Adonis.

'The subscriber you have dialed is no longer available' the operator spoke in his ear. "Fuck," he said instantly getting pissed. "This nigga must of changed his number." Truth thought to himself.

"Here you go sir.", the nurse said leaving the Percocet's on the table for Truth to take with a cup of water. Deciding it was nothing for him do for now, he took his medication and closed his eyes to get some rest. About an hour later, Truth felt like someone was watching him. Opening his eyes, he saw Derrick watching him from beside his bed.

"Well, well, well," Derrick said staring at Truth.

"Nigga get the fuck out of my room before I call security!" Truth warned searching frantically for the nurse button.

"I just came to talk." Derrick replied. "I think we have a misunderstanding. Now I sent you to handle a drop for me 4 days ago, and the money never reached my account but you knew that didn't you Truth?" Derrick questioned as he pulled his gun out laying it on the bed near Truths foot. "So what happened to the money I was supposed to get from the drop? And don't you lie to me motherfucker or I'll kill your ass so fast you won't be able to see your maker fast enough!"

Truth whispered, "Nigga I put the money in your safe and the rest in both of your off shore accounts, so I don't know what the fuck you talking about!" He didn't have time to bullshit around with Derrick or hear any of his threats.

"Look nigga ain't nobody stupid. I know you been stealing money from me! You tried to frame Louie but I figured it out. You and Adonis been trying to play me." Derrick hissed.

"Nigga you are really as dumb as you look. What the

hell would me and Adonis have to gain from trying to steal from your ass? If we were that dirty, we would have tried to kill your ass off a long time ago. Second of all, your son is the reason why I'm in this hospital bed. I'm pretty sure he never gonna speak to me again, so get the hell out of here accusing me of some foul shit old man." Troy spatt back.

"Why he ain't speaking to you?" Derrick wondered curiously.

"Because he not! It's none of your business!" Truth responded fumbling with phone in his hand.

"Nigga you need to man up you acting like you lost your bitch or something." Derrick said noticing the shift in his mood at the mention of Adonis. Truth didn't respond.

"Oh my God, you mothafucka!!!" Derrick yelled finally realizing what it was. "Nigga you want my son don't you?" Derrick stated more than asking him. "I knew your ass was sweeter than a chocolate sundae from Shoneys!" Derrick shook his head. Truth held his down in shame. He hated that people in the hood would never understand or respect the fact that he was gay. He couldn't help the fact that he was attracted to or fell in love with Adonis. It was just something that happened.

This was the prime example of why he never wanted Derrick or any of the men in The Dynasty to find out his secret. They automatically would size him up as being a weak ass faggot who got into his feelings too much. They would think that he was a pussy nigga which he was far from it. Which was why planned to still deny his feeling for Adonis to anybody on the streets, especially since he knew they would probably never be together now.

"I don't know what type of shit you on or drug you smoking, but you heard wrong. Ain't nobody gay!" Truth stated trying to act as if he was offended.

"Truth I been hearing for a good minute that you like a little swirl in your coffee. This ain't no new news that

I just got in my dm or heard on the street. Look I don't give a fuck about you being gay, but you won't be pressing up on my son with that shit. He was born to love the pussy and he ain't going out on no soft shit like that. So fall back and that's my final warning Truth! Now you probably done saved yourself for now, but imma find out what really happened to my money and if I find out that it's not in one of my offshore accounts like you said, imma bust a cap in your ass I don't play about my damn money!" Derrick threatened him as he grabbed his gun and rolled out of Truths hospital room.

Truth was sweating bullets. He couldn't believe that Derrick thought him and Adonis was taking money from him. True it was just him, but why would he suspect Adonis? The shit was crazy. He knew that he had to think fast before he ended up getting killed. He was sure that he had been secure in the moves he had made, but lately he was starting to realize that he was becoming messy. Louie body ended up being found, and now he had to cover up the fact that he had been stealing the money from Derrick for the past year and a half.

"Damn I gotta get out this hospital bed." Truth muttered. The only thing on his mind was getting Adonis back and trying to get away from Derrick King before he ended up 10 feet under.

Chapter 21

Adonis finally finished at Shawn's place. He had gotten rid of the body and made sure the place was spotless. He then made a few calls and set up a flight for Imani and him to leave Chicago in the morning. Even though it took up his whole day it was worth it. Him and his girl could finally leave the hood behind and progress and go forward. He knew that he had put Imani through enough, and that one more fuck up might cause her to walk away. He would never be able to get over the fact that had he not thrown her over at Shawn's house, she wouldn't have gotten raped. It was mentally fucking with him. The only thing left for him to do was throw his old cellphone away. He had already stopped by Verizon to have the services canceled. He wanted to make it look as if him and Imani had dropped off the face of the earth.

Pulling into his driveway, he cut off the car and sat inside just thinking about his momma. She looked just like him and was beautiful. Even though it was only a minute he shared with her, it felt like a lifetime. He had made a vow to himself to make sure that he would find her when he reached New York. He had to know the truth about why she abandoned him all of those years ago. He knew they would have to be low key when they went to the big apple, but he would have to take that chance. Adonis was tired of feeling like the kid who grew up with adopted parents, and wanted just to have a moment with his biological parents. He craved for his momma more than a bond with his pops. That bothered him to the core, especially since Derrick had been there to raise him his whole life. That void that he felt couldn't be filled until he found out the truth.

Walking into the house, he called out Imani's name. She was in the room sitting on the edge of the bed crying.

"What's wrong baby?" he asked concerned.

"I just feel so dead inside." Imani replied. "I never knew I could feel so dirty. It feels like I cheated on you having another nigga fuck me raw instead of you." She cried. The pain that she felt was so strong and ran deep to her core. She didn't know why she felt like she cheated on Adonis, but she did. She had tried her best to forget about Shawn raping her but all it did was bring back the images from when her foster mother and father had molested her. Not knowing what to tell her, Adonis held her in his arms so tight. He just wanted her to feel safe again and to understand that no matter what he would never let her be in danger or harms away again. He was gonna make her his wife and protect her for the rest of his life. She would never have to worry about being alone afraid. It was his life mission to put her first and make her happy.

"Imani when we get to New York I wanna make you my wife." He said pulling the box out of his pocket with a huge diamond ring inside.

"Baby," she replied shocked that he finally asked. Getting on knee he looked her in the eyes and spoke. "Imani you are my hope, my future, my sun, and my dream. Before I met you, all a nigga knew was the streets. I felt lost and incomplete and unsure If I would ever find a woman that would make me wanna change my life. Then I met you," he said wiping the tears from her beautiful caramel skin. "You came into my world and convinced me that it was more to life than being a drug pin more than wasting my life away by catering to my fathers every demand. With you, you have shown me courage and shown me the true definition in what being strong truly is. You made me wanna be a better man, will you marry me Imani?"

"Yes I will baby I do I do!!!" She cried hugging me so tightly. Finally, after going on 6 years of dating he was making her his number one.

She thought he would never ask. Putting the beautiful diamond carat ring on her finger, she was amazed at how heavy it was to be only an engagement ring.

"Do you like it?" Adonis asked.

"I love it". Imani replied not able to take her eyes off of it. I have everything taken care of so we can leave for New York tomorrow. I need you to pack lightly and call and cancel your cellphone plan. We will get a new everything once we get settled in New York." Adonis explained.

"Can I at least call Nyla before we leave?" Imani asked. She hated the thought of having to leave her best friend behind.

"Yes you can. Imma try to get it taken care of to where you don't have to cut Nyla off. I know she like family to you baby." He promised.

"Okay," she said kissing him on the lips. "Baby thank you for keeping your word and changing your life, for not just me but for us. I know these past couple of years haven't been easy, but I do love you. I thought you would never be able to give up The Dynasty for me. I always knew that you loved me, but for so long I questioned how deep did that love run. You have proved that you are more than worthy of becoming my husband. You should already know how we rocking and that you shouldn't even have to ask for me to marry you, because I would do it in a heartbeat." She said holding his hands and brushing his face.

His eyes said it all he looked like the happiest man in the world. Even his skin was dark chocolate he was glowing. "Imani I just want us to focus on life as we know it now. For what it is, fuck our past, our mistakes, and our pain. Giving her the new Id and social security card, he made sure she understood that from here on out things would be better.

"Starting next week, this will be us when we get off

that plane and land in New York. We won't be Imani and Adonis. We will be new people with hopefully a new life far from worry or pain."

"You promise?" she said.

"I give you my word baby," he said kissing her passionately. Breaking the kiss, she stopped herself.

"I can't do this... I'm not ready Adonis." she said still thinking of what happened with Shawn.

"It's okay baby. We can take our time. Can I just hold you for tonight?" he asked.

"Now you know in your arms is where I would love to be." She smiled as they laid next to each other in the bed. Holding her hand and cuddling her in his arms, he felt so much at peace. It was just them and the soft slow jams playing in the background. For the very first time in a long time, things felt normal and right. Imani had been feeling so discouraged with Adonis, but after he proposed she knew that now the bond that they shared could only get stronger. Nothing in this lifetime could change the course of what was to come for them. Tonight they would lay up in love and peace until the sun came up.

Chapter 22

Finally jumping out the shower, Imani was finally ready to start her new journey with her fiancé' Adonis. Her and Adonis were leaving Chicago tonight. They were gonna change their names and start over. The whole 9. Imani hated to leave Chicago, but she knew if they stayed here one of them would end up in jail or dead. Throwing on her clothes and packing up the last of her belongings, she yelled down for Adonis to hurry up. Their flight to New York would be leaving out in the next two hours.

"Bae you almost done?" Imani yelled.

Adonis rushed up the stairs. The Uber would be there to pick them up in about 15 minutes. Adonis was gonna miss all of his cars, but he could rebuild once they got up north. They couldn't take anything with them it would make it look to obvious

Hearing her phone ring Imani saw it was Nyla calling.

"Hey!" Imani answered. "We about to be out." She said sadly. Imani had been talking on the phone with her friend since early this morning. Nyla was so happy that Adonis had finally proposed. She knew that it would be a matter of time before he would decide not to let her get away. Imani couldn't lie, she was gonna miss the hell out of Nyla. The whole time they had been friends, she always doubted Nyla's loyalty. When shit had hit the fan, Nyla didn't go to the police. Yes, she has been mad at her for friend for lying, but at the same time who was she to judge? In the end, she still loved her. No matter what the circumstances were Nyla was gonna ride for Imani. For sure Imani could put trust in her after everything she had taken Nyla through.

"Girl I got something to tell you. I'm pregnant."

Nyla sighed. Nyla had finally worked up the nerve to let her girl know. She couldn't hold water, and it felt so much better telling someone what she was going through.

"Awwwww," Imani was so happy for her friend. She didn't sound too excited.

"Are you gonna keep it?" Imani asked hoping she would say yes.

"I'm not sure," Nyla said. "I asked Troy to move out and told him I need my space. He just wants to much from me right now, and I don't know if I will ever be able to forgive him for how he did me. He doesn't know about the baby. I just think we need some space and time apart. If I have this baby, I won't have anyone by my side with you gone." Nyla broke down in tears.

"It won' t always be this way." Imani promised her friend. "After we get settled in New York, imma contact you from my new number. I promise just don't make any decisions yet Nyla. You promise?" Imani pleaded.

"I promise." Nyla replied wiping her face. "Love you Imani," she said hanging up the phone. Holding the phone to her chest, she hated she had to leave Nyla behind. Not forgetting to call the phone company, she quickly canceled her phone plan. It was bittersweet. Imani had that phone number ever since she moved to Chicago. Feeling a bit sad, she had to remember to boss up and keep telling herself that she was making the right decision.

"Babe the Uber is here." Adonis yelled up the stairs. Grabbing her small duffel bag and her purse, she gave Adonis the last of her belongings to be packed into the Uber. She couldn't believe after 5 and a half years, she was leaving the one place that she called home for so many years. Deep down in Imani's heart, she knew that wherever Adonis was would always be a place she could call home in her heart. Packing the last of their things, Adonis helped Imani into the back seat of the Uber. Placing her head on his shoulder she finally felt at peace. No more Truth or Derrick. No more drugs or murders. Just a happy new life for her and Adonis.

She couldn't wait to see what the future may hold.

"Where ya'll headed to?" The Uber driver asked.

"The O'Hare International." Adonis replied.

"I'm saying my man where you headed to? Why leave the great city of Chi-Town baby?" The man chuckled adjusting his shades in the driver's seat.

"We going to New York City." Imani replied. Adonis nudged her. He didn't want nobody to know where they were going. If they were gonna leave Chicago and start fresh, Imani couldn't just run her mouth like normal. They had to keep everything air-tight. Seeing the signs for the airport, Imani started to get excited. She had never been on a plane and couldn't wait to be relaxing amongst the clouds with her boo.

"Hey sir, the exit for O'Hare was on the right," Imani tapped him on the shoulder.

"Don't worry Ms. Lady. I'm just taking a little shortcut," The driver replied.

"Aye man, we just wanna get to the airport. We don't have a lot time to be taking detours." Adonis told him firmly.

"Well son how we gonna go The Big Apple without picking up my bags?" The driver said adjusting the mirror so they could both see his face. The driver took off his shades. Adonis couldn't believe his eyes, and Imani looked as if she had seen a ghost.

"Now my son, did you really think you could leave your old man all alone in the Chi Town!!??" Derrick replied laughing hysterically as he pressed his foot on the gas speeding off in the SUV.

"Buckle up son and daughter-in-law, we in for a long ride!!"

To Be Continued

CPSIA information can be obtained
at www.ICGtesting.com
Printed in the USA
LVOW12s1628310517
536450LV00013B/642/P